PAPER BOATS &
BUTTERFLIES

Unfolding the Truth

Sue Upton

Illustrations by Becky Stewart

Sue Upton
info@sueupton-author.com
First Published: May 2019
Second Edition: October 2021
by
Budding Authors Assistant
www.help2publish.co.uk
Illustrations by Becky Stewart
Cover design by Lauren Zorkoczy

ISBN:- 9781919625430

Paper Boats & Butterflies Trilogy

Unfolding the Truth… (Book 1)

True Tears (Book 2)

Igniting the Truth… (Book 3)

To Chris, Josh and Fred.

Chapter 1

Z89 stood in the centre of the stone cell, the cold slabs hard against her bare feet. In the gloom, her smoky eyes became aware of small movements in the shadowy corners of the room. A scratching and rustling to her right made her turn her head. Holding her breath as something soft and warm slid over her feet, she folded her fingers into tight fists.

Rats.

She swallowed and breathed in deeply to calm her nerves. No weakness could be shown - that was unseemly.

As the overhead lights became brighter huge black spiders appeared squeezing through the lightning shaped cracks in the walls and stretching out their long, articulated legs towards her. The girl forced herself to keep her eyes open and to stare at the huge seething mass before her. It won't be long now, she thought to herself.

A rat with sharp protruding teeth began making its way towards her. Then the others followed.

Black and brown slivers of fur scratched their way menacingly across the stone floor and began to tear at her feet, her legs. The spiders whispered across the stone and tangled their sticky webs around her skinny body. Z89 tried to scream but no sound came out. She started to kick at the horde of biting rodents, of the tangle of legs and hooked mouths of the arachnids, but to no avail. More followed - biting, gnawing, scratching.

"Please make them stop!" Her voice came now as a shout. Taking a deep breath Z89 screamed – a shrill painful sound that pierced the air. Then as she felt she was going to pass out, the lights were slammed off. Z89 fell to the ground panting, her chest heaving for oxygen.

Moments later, the stark white lights clicked back on.

No rats, no spiders, just a girl in grey lying on a white tiled floor.

"Work always comes first. I hate you!" Erin punctuated her final sentence with a slam of the front door.

She stomped down the winding, gravel driveway to the main gates and angrily pushed one open. They don't love me, she thought. They can't even be around for my fifteenth birthday! I'm a huge disappointment and they don't care about me or anything I do. Erin rubbed her hand across her eyes smudging the black eye liner that adorned them. I will not cry.

Rounding the corner of the road she automatically glanced right and left, even though this was a cul-de-sac and very few vehicles came this way, then crossed quickly. Ignoring the other select houses that also hugged the hill where her family home looked out across the town, head firmly down, a curtain of raven black hair protecting her, the young girl trudged on. Erin finally came to the end of the road and turned into the large field that lay ahead. Stopping and finally lifting her head, she breathed in deeply. Her safe place – The Place of the Seven Spirits.

She stumbled through the long wavy grasses towards a raised area where a flat, octagonal stone overlooked the more upright stones standing as silent sentinels waiting. Clambering on to the rocky altar and drawing her knees tightly to her chest, Erin finally let out a huge sigh of relief. This was a special spot for her. She always felt calm here, amongst the rocky remnants of outcasts from the medieval village that had once spread across the hillside. She too, often endured being an outcast, an outsider. Here she could put things into perspective. Families – who'd have them? she thought to herself.

She hadn't meant to say the things she said but sometimes …

Her mum had called out to her as she arrived home from school. "Good day, darling?"

Erin flung her bag against a fat, grey sofa and threw herself onto the opposite identical one. The softness of the cushions gave her comfort after another horrendous day at school. She slumped down after grabbing the remote, flicking through channels, ignoring her mum. The question floated in the air unanswered as Stella Winslow, a tall attractive woman in her forties with short bobbed hair, entered the large comfortable lounge and leaned over to kiss her daughter.

"So?" Stella asked, sitting gracefully down

opposite Erin. She crossed her lean limbs elegantly and waited, drumming pointed pink nails on the side of the chair, staring across at her daughter and sighing deeply.

"So, what?" Erin asked.

"How was school?"

In answer, Erin rummaged in her pocket and threw a crumpled letter at her mother. Stella scanned the note. "Detention? Not again, darling. That's three times this term already."

"I didn't know you were counting," Erin replied, frowning.

Now, a few hours later, she rubbed her hands together to warm them against the cool air of the early evening. She didn't know how long she'd sat there, time seemed to stop when she was here. The seven spirits stood watching her, guarding the slight girl in the oversized black leather jacket. Erin had just grabbed what was nearest the door in her rush to leave the house and realised too late she had her brother, Mal's jacket instead. She pulled the collar up against the cold and burrowed down into its warmth; voices and images from earlier whizzing around her head.

The argument had flared once the detention letter struck the light of her mother's mood. Soon they were at loggerheads and everything Erin had held tight in her head, all her pain, frustration and anger came tumbling out. What had been a tiny flame burning inside her now became an enormous flare of frustration.

Over dinner, nobody had spoken, until her dad and Malachi began discussing university and whether he was going to take maths or physics. Patrick then turned to Erin and innocently enquired how her maths exam had gone. Her poor dad didn't know he'd reignited the fire. Suddenly, Erin was shouting at him and as her voice rose, so did his. Before she knew it, there were sparks flying between them all. Everything that had lain dormant in her mind now awoke - school was awful - she was trying so hard to improve but she got distracted easily and then got into trouble, she was late for lessons and school in the morning and now some of her friends were ignoring her too.

As she stood to leave the family dinner table, she threw her final irritation and hurt at her parents and brother – nobody cared about her. They only cared about themselves and Mal – the perfect son, the perfect student and she was a huge disappointment to them all.

"I can't believe you are going to be away for my birthday. You never miss good old Malachi's birthday, do you? No, of course not, he's your favourite! When do I come first?" Erin dramatically held her clenched fist against her chest at this point. Stella looked at her husband at this outburst and Patrick glowered at his daughter. Erin continued. "No, he's perfect isn't he. Never in trouble. Not like me. Well I'm glad you'll be away. I hate you."

Alone and cold, feeling sorry for herself, Erin hugged her legs tightly. Her mum had threatened her with moving schools. Erin didn't want to move to Saint Luke's ten miles away, she was happy where she was. *If only Mum and Dad noticed when I did something well instead of just seeing all the mistakes I make.*

The watery sun slipped soundlessly towards the horizon over the tangled streets of the town; the orange, pink glow seeped higher and higher to become a watercolour painting. Erin sighed and took a photo with her phone; perhaps she could use those colours in her next art piece.

Suddenly a light flashed from behind one of the standing stones and a gruff voice cried out, "I can see you." Erin jumped as she saw a ghostly apparition rise above the granite. For a moment she couldn't breathe. The apparition seemed to beckon to her, and she shrank back against the limestone altar stone. "Erin, come to me." The voice became even more shrill. "Come to me now." Then a hacking cough caused the apparition to double over and the light rolled away.

"Petra! Is that you?" Erin peered again through the misty darkness and now could make out a fluffy bobble-hatted person in a dark coat. The figure stopped coughing and made their way towards Erin.

"Spooked you, didn't I?" Petra said flopping down next to her Erin.

"Hardly!" exclaimed Erin. "I knew it was you by your ridiculous hat." She grabbed the pink bobble hat and pulled it over her friend's face.

Inseparable since they had started school together, they had both been four, and were delighted to find out they shared a birthday. The two girls were very different - Petra had blonde hair in contrast to Erin's black and Petra could make anyone laugh while Erin was always on a downer - but they complemented each other. Their interests were different too – karate and drawing for Erin and dancing and science for Petra.

Erin began to silently weep. "Hey, what's this?" Petra asked. "What is it now?" Erin's tears fell and as they splashed down onto her jeans, Petra pulled her towards her.

Gradually, Erin found the tears began to slow. Sniffing, she pulled a scrunched-up tissue from her jeans pocket. "Another argument," she stuttered nasally. "It's no good. I'm no good. No one cares, I may as well top myself."

Petra rubbed Erin's back. "You don't mean that." They had gone through this so many times. Erin shared her thoughts with Petra like before - she always felt she never came up to the high expectations of her parents, always felt her brother,

Malachi, was the favourite and always felt second best. Erin explained that her parents thought she should concentrate on improving her grades in the 'important subjects' and not follow her love for art and designing.

"I don't know any more, perhaps this time I do mean it. They might sit up and take notice if I did." Erin pulled at the tissue absentmindedly, creating snowy flakes that the evening wind caught and blew away. She wished the wind could blow her cares away just as easily.

"Hey, it's snowing up here!" A voice floated towards them.

"I wish it could be Christmas every day!" sang another, the notes going low and then high. Other voices joined in then. As Erin and Petra looked over to the entrance of the field, shadowy figures began to materialise through the evening mist.

"Happy Christmas – ho ho ho!" shouted Roberto, one of the boys in the group, his long black leather-look coat dragging across the tall grass as he strode towards them.

"It's February, you idiot!" Petra's voice was full of smiles. Erin heard her friend laugh and found herself smiling as the rest of the crew arrived and flung themselves down on the dampening grass.

"What are you doing out here?" Elsa, a moon-faced girl with the straightest, longest hair Erin had ever seen, asked. "It's freezing." She pulled her red woollen jacket tightly around her slightly plump body to emphasise her point.

"Just passing the time of day," replied Petra. She glanced at Erin who was already beginning to feel brighter. "What about you?"

Nadir cleared his throat, "We're revising for our biology test by studying the human form in the natural setting of …" he gestured wildly, "… of the flora and fauna of the archetypal British countryside." His voice had taken on the accent of David Attenborough. Erin giggled as he walked over to her. "As you can see, this is the lesser spotted Erinitis Winslow-bird, often observed in detention. Also, it follows the mating call of Shay of the wild." At this Erin punched him hard on the arm. Shay was a boy at school she'd 'admired' for a long time.

"Yes, and if angered she'll attack you forcefully and accurately with a few kicks and punches." Erin suppressed a giggle as she aimed the perfect karate kick at Nadir's head, stopping short by a few millimetres.

"Lethal and deadly when riled." Nadir perched himself on one of the Spirit rocks he knew when to stop. Sitting hunched over, just like Gollum, he began to stare wildly around, slapping his lips together. He rubbed his hands and started laughing like a drain, before he was unceremoniously pushed off his throne by Rob.

The others all burst out laughing as Nadir fell

into a heap.

"Where's Willow?" asked Petra.

"Still doing her make-up," answered Rob, groaning. His girlfriend was never on time to anything. Again, they laughed as they all knew how much time their friend spent on looking just right.

Erin was beginning to feel much better. They were a good group of friends who had been through a lot over the years since they all started at the local primary school.

"Anyway, how's the show going, Nad?" Rob stretched himself out on the altar stone, his big brown Doc Martens dangling over one end. "What is it again? Shakespeare?"

"We're doing High School Musical, and I hate it." Nadir wanted to go to drama school, but much preferred plays to musicals. He stood, placing one hand on his hip and the other hand outstretched. "We should be doing Hamlet. To be or not to be, that is the question." The others applauded and called for more. Just as he was about to, Willow arrived. Her red, screw curled hair shone in the street lights that were just coming on. Rob went to meet her, and they walked back together holding hands.

Erin envied them. Would I ever be like that with Shay? she wondered. Looking around at the others, all of them chatting, for a moment she saw herself as a stranger standing outside looking in. Even when she was with her friends she was always on the periphery of the group – that familiar ache came again to her chest of something missing from her life and a longing to be loved and accepted.

Later as she and Petra trudged home after they had all gone their separate ways, Erin thanked her friend for being there for her. She knew she needed to be strong now and go and apologise to everyone. Petra hugged her and turned in towards her house; she waved as she disappeared down the long driveway.

The house looked cold and dark apart from one single light glowing from her mother's study window, as Erin let herself in. She kicked off her boots and crept up the stairs. The study door was slightly ajar, and Erin could hear her mum talking on the phone.

"I don't know what to do with her." Erin heard her saying and realised she was being discussed here. She paused before knocking, holding her breath, afraid her mum would know she was eavesdropping.

"I love her so much, and I want to tell her, but it's forbidden. It's 2015, we've lasted for fifteen years now. She deserves to know." Stella went quiet, obviously listening to the voice on the other end. Erin took in a sharp breath and sniffed. Stella spun round in her chair. "Erin ... how long have you been there?" Putting the phone down, she went to lower her lap top in front of her, but Erin was too quick and coming up to the desk saw a picture of herself on the screen. She was sitting on a grey sofa, in a pink dress with her dark hair curled softly around her face.

"Mum, that's an awful picture of me. What have you done to it? I never wear pink."

Stella Winslow looked aghast at Erin's comments.

"I know what you're up to." Erin said.

"You do?" Stella raised her eyebrows and looked pointedly at her daughter.

Erin laughed then. "You've been playing with the colour effects on the screen." Stella breathed out slowly. "Mum, I am not a sugar and spice and all things nice kind of girl. Stop trying to put me in pink!"

Erin stared at her mother. She realised she'd been crying; her mascara streaked through her foundation. "I'm sorry, Mum – I didn't mean to upset you and … I'm sorry for my behaviour earlier."

"Oh, Erin. I'm sorry too," Stella said as she rose quickly and hugged her daughter close.

Erin knew she should be more appreciative. She lived in an amazing house; she had good friends and yes, she admitted to herself, her parents loved her just as much as her brother. They just weren't very good at showing it. Mum and Dad were always under a lot of pressure through their work. At times they seemed distant and uncaring and yet there were good times. The many holidays abroad, the wonderful presents, the birthday parties … and then she remembered they would be away for this one. The same old worries began to cloud her thoughts again.

"Mum. Can I ask you something?"

"Yes, what is it darling?" Stella Winslow gently lifted some of the black veil of hair that had fallen across her daughter's face and hooked it behind a tiny silver-studded ear.

"Am I adopted?"

Stella sighed. "No, Erin, you are not adopted. You are ours. I love you and always will, whatever happens." She pulled Erin close to her again. "I'm sorry we will be away for your birthday, but we'll make it up to you. We could go to London for the day when we get back perhaps. Do some shopping, see a show, go and eat at the Hard Rock café. What do you think?"

Erin nodded. "That would be good. Thank you. I love you too, Mum."

Erin wandered across to her bedroom and reflected on the phone conversation. Who had been on the phone? More importantly though, what could be forbidden and what did Mum want to tell me? Erin was determined to find out more.

Chapter 2

"The electric shock treatment you received last week while studying pictures of rats and spiders created this disturbance in your mind. You are now terrified of them." The voice emitted from the speakers in the room. Once the bright lights had come back on, Z89 was told to exit and then go through into the next chamber where she found one solitary table and one hard metal chair.

The voice went on. "The second part of this experiment is for you to write down all the emotions you felt while you were in the Sensory Chamber. What did you feel, see, hear, taste, smell?"

There was a piece of white paper on the table and a pen. "Could I have a pencil please? I prefer to write in pencil." The silent guard standing to attention by the door ignored her. Then a small door set in the wall, clicked open and a tiny pencil rolled onto the floor.

"Thank you." The girl began to write, reliving her experiences. As she did so, the sweat began to pour out of her, the tears dripped onto the table and the paper. She wiped her damp hands on to her grey leggings several times.

"That will be all for today, Z89 Marcon."

The slight, slim girl stood. She absentmindedly scratched at her razor cut hair while she waited patiently. The side door opened, and the guard motioned for her to move.

Outside the chamber, Z89 walked uncomfortably, as though she was in pain, down the narrow, brightly lit corridor. She turned into the Nod Pod section and quickly found her bay. The walls were white with inbuilt ladders at regular intervals. Small square windows sat one on top of the other next to the ladders. Climbing one stiffly, she pressed a blue button and a window slid open. Z89 gratefully climbed into her bunk. There she finally relaxed. She pulled up her grey T shirt and gently pulled out the pencil hidden in the waistband of her leggings. Then Z89 tucked it in a crack between the mattress and the wall.

 "How long's Grandma staying?" Erin asked her mother as she watched her flitting from the bedroom to the huge walk-in wardrobe, carrying clothes and a case.

"Only a few days, until we get back darling." Stella looked up as Erin perched herself on the edge of the king-sized bed. "It won't be for long, then we can celebrate together. Grandma and Malachi will be with you."

"It's not the same though is it?" Erin sighed. "I suppose I'm just getting older and that's what happens; birthdays aren't so important."

"Your birthdays will always be important to us. You are important to us Erin, just as Malachi is. Petra could come over if you want. You've always said you would like to celebrate together. Now's your chance."

Erin continued to watch her mother folding designer clothes into the suitcase.

"You look like you're going away for ever, Mum. Do you really need all those clothes?"

"Well, you know me. I never know what to wear."

"Just work clothes surely," Erin said as her mum piled in a long evening dress.

Stella stopped and looked at Erin. "Well, there's evening things too you know. Business conferences aren't all boring lectures. Anyway, your dad and I may as well enjoy ourselves if we have to be away together in a four-star hotel." She folded and tucked, and then squashed things into her case. "Haven't you got anything better to do than watch me? How about that maths homework? Have you done that yet?"

Erin sighed and slid off her parents' comfortable bed. She knew when she wasn't wanted.

Later, in her bedroom, after making a milky coffee and grabbing a pile of biscuits, Erin sat staring out the window. She could just about see the Seven Spirits, in the field beyond, sitting there waiting for her presence. Maths equations floated off the paper as she looked down at her book that lay open on the desk; her eyes began crossing over themselves. Erin rubbed her eyes and then worked through some of the questions, but it was painfully slow and tedious. So many things in her room tried to distract her – tantalising art books piled high at the back of her desk beckoned her to study images of long-gone artists; an impatient phone beeping every few minutes with messages and images to make her laugh; a cosy bed piled high with cushions inviting her to sleep.

Looking up again, trying to make sense of the numbers that seemed to dance in front of her, she glanced again at the seven rocks standing there at the top of the hill overlooking the town of Newton. Laying down her pen, and taking up her mug of coffee, Erin thought about the mystery of how they got there.

The legend was there had been seven young men and women who used to meet to dance and sing together. They were seen as being different from the rest of the village. Each one had been touched by the devil, or so the other villagers believed – one was blind in one eye, another walked with a limp, another flicked his head from side to side. Back then no one understood illness or disabilities. The women in the group were intelligent and would question the elders of the village; this was not allowed. Women were treated as inferior to men because they lacked the ability to think or act responsibly. The elders would pray in church for God to take them away, to cleanse the village.

Erin felt sorry for these people. She and her friends were all different, and just like these shadows from the Dark Ages, they didn't conform either. She remembered learning all about the strangers from the past at the junior school on the other side of the town; Erin loved going there every day, unlike Newton Academy which she now attended. She remembered her favourite teacher, Miss Chaucer, encouraged her to draw and paint and would sit them down on the carpet in front of her comfy chair and tell them stories.

According to the legend, these seven people were dancing on the Sabbath when a raging thunder storm rose up and a huge lightning bolt crackled down on them showering them all with the might of God. They were immediately turned to stone and became known as the Seven Spirits. During the storm a huge rock appeared, the rain washing away the earth that covered it. The elders agreed this would be the altar for the Spirits to worship God for eternity. Erin shivered as she looked out at a place of such sad memories and yet, for her, it was a place of peace.

Memories were something Erin treasured, mostly in picture form on her phone – silly pictures of her and Petra and the rest of the crew. She had pictures of family birthdays, Christmases and holidays all there stored inside a tiny metal and glass rectangle. Her mum loved using a camera and only had a very old mobile phone. She always said, "I just need it to make phone calls and nothing else." Her dad, in complete contrast, loved technology and enjoyed nothing better than outdoing his children with a better phone than them.

Erin suddenly remembered the picture she'd seen on her mum's lap top. Knocking back the final drops of coffee, and placing her empty mug on the desk, she thought I wonder if it's in one of my albums? Going over to the very full bookcase that towered above her, she knelt onto the sheepskin rug that lay before it and tugged her photo albums from the bottom shelf. Her mum added to her birthday album every year - the same place, same time each year since her birth. Other albums stored images of special events in her life. One album was made up of pictures of Erin being presented at karate gradings with a new belt, each time a different colour, until the final one - a black belt – the highest honour to achieve.

Erin pulled open one of the albums. Inside there were pictures of all her previous birthdays with Mum and Dad and Mal; each year a different cake and a different hair style. Her lovely grandma and grandad were often in the pictures too; Dinah and Marcus Trent. They were her mum's parents and lived over in Norfolk near to the sea, in a little cottage with roses growing wildly around the front door. Erin loved to spend time with them. Sadly, her dad's parents died long ago, Silas and Joyce Winslow. She didn't remember them very well at all, they were just distant shadows in her life.

Leafing through the years, one photograph came loose and floated lazily to the floor. Erin stretched to pick it up – it landed face down – just like buttered toast always did. She smiled at this and then paused before sticking it back onto the page that announced – Erin's 10th Birthday. A date was printed on the back – automatically recorded by the camera on the day of the photograph being taken. 3.3.10. That's strange, Erin thought. I was sure these were always taken on my actual birthday. She flipped it over and there they all were smiling into the camera with the birthday cake. It had balloons all over it as she loved the film Up! The candles were lit, Erin was smiling, her hair was slicked back with a lilac coloured hair band and she wore a dress of purple velvet with tiny silver stars cascading down.

Sticking the picture back in, she wondered about that birthday, only five years ago, and yet she couldn't remember much of it. Then a sudden image came to her, of her mother climbing in beside her dad into the back of a taxi as her grandma held her hand tightly, telling her to smile and wave to her parents. They baked some biscuits that day – Erin could remember licking the icing from the bowl and feeling quite sick afterwards. Her birthday had been a normal school day; Miss Chaucer encouraged the class to sing to her and Petra, while they sat wearing the 'birthday princess crowns' and then they stood at the door, at the end of the day, handing out sweets to their friends.

Erin remembered now the awful hollow feeling that had remained until her parents came home. On their return they plied her with presents, all beautifully wrapped. Being together again and all the gifts, including the much-wanted Go-Go toy hamster, took her mind off her parents' trip away and it was all forgotten and they were forgiven.

Having sat for a long time, pins and needles began to fizz in her feet and Erin stretched out her legs wiggling her toes to bring back the circulation. How could I forget Hammy? thought Erin. Whatever happened to him? Another image swam into her thoughts and she sighed. Oh, yeah, Mal threw it out of the top window as a science experiment and his parachute failed to open. Hammy is no more! Looking down at the picture before her, there was Hammy at her belated birthday tea, the only image she had of him. Erin smiled. "Rest in peace, Hammy," she whispered.

What other things do I remember about my birthdays? she thought. Erin began to look back at the previous pictures, enjoying the memories of long-lost toys, all the while checking the dates on the back - all were 1st March until she arrived at her fifth birthday.

3.3.05. Another late picture.

This time the cake was Lazy Town and there was Erin dressed in … pink! She gasped. I did like pink. How could I forget? I had loved that dress – it was just like the one worn by the girl in the programme - pink and white stripes. What was her name? Erin cast her mind back – Stephanie - and she had pink hair too. She remembered saying to her parents she wanted pink hair like that. Subsequently Erin painted her Barbie's hair with pink poster paint. Her mum was furious, especially as she'd also hacked most of it off too!

Continuing with her search, Erin turned the pages, carefully removing the pictures and checking the date. It wasn't until she came back to the beginning of the album, that she found another discrepancy. There was a lovely picture of Erin on her first birthday; all toothy smiles and tiny hands grabbing for the icing and this one had 3.3.01 on the back.

Strange, Erin thought to herself. Why were the pictures taken two days late? Were her parents away for those birthdays? She suddenly laughed. This is ridiculous, it's just coincidence. But 1, 5, 10 and now 15. Erin pushed the albums back on to the shelf and stood, brushing fluff from her jeans. "I will talk it through with Petra," she announced to the empty room. She would tell me what a load of nonsense this is. Anyway, I'm old enough now to enjoy a party with just friends, who needs parents anyway! Erin laughed as she texted her friend and arranged to meet later that evening.

Petra was waiting at the Seven Spirits, sitting with her back against one of the upright stones. She looks fed up, thought Erin as she walked steadily towards her. As Erin's shadow fell across the blonde girl's face, she looked up. Her eyes were red from crying. Erin threw herself down onto the soft, mossy grass and hugged Petra.

"They're going to be away for my birthday too," Petra said sniffing loudly. "Mum and Dad have said they have to go away this weekend."

"Oh well, we will just have to celebrate without them. We could come up here and bring some wine and stuff. That's what I've decided to do for my birthday. We're not little any more. We can do what we want!" Erin said kicking off her Vans. She picked at the clover leaves that were pushing up between the blades of grass. It was mild for a February evening, but the sun was slowly sinking towards the horizon and the air was becoming cooler. Birds sang in the trees and a lone robin perched on one of the stones. Erin felt at peace for a few moments, but then turned to her friend who was now searching through messages on her phone.

"Do you know what I think is really weird?"

"No. What?" Petra responded.

"I was looking through pictures of previous birthdays. My parents weren't around for my 1st, 5th and my 10th. We celebrated after the actual day."

Petra looked across at Erin. "Parents are useless aren't they. They're never around when you need them"

"True, but why every five years? And now they're away for my 15th. I think that's weird."

Petra started scrolling through the photos on her phone. She was very good at recording every minute of the day and quickly came to her birthdays file. Erin sat there listening to the silence of the space around them, the birds had quietened, and the robin had flown away. A thin, weakened sun was trying to send rays of copper through the grey clouds as it hit the edge of the world. She too, began to scroll through pictures on her phone. Photos of the many sunsets she'd seen from this spot. Standing up, she flicked to camera and shot images of the evening sky as it changed from orange to pink to slate grey. She shivered then. A sense of foreboding crept around her like a thief stealing her moments of peace.

"Me too," Petra said abruptly. Erin spun round and stared at the girl sitting on the grass before her. Shadows peered over her and for a second, Erin saw her friend's face seem to change, her eyes darkened, and her cheeks hollowed. She looked dead. Erin gasped but then as the light on Petra's phone shone brightly again, she came back to life.

"They weren't around for my tenth either." She continued scrolling. Over the years Petra had moved various photos from cameras and laptops on to her phone. "Same for my fifth and my first. Spooky or what?"

Erin walked across to the altar stone and perching herself on the edge she began to think about what she'd just seen and heard. Petra clambered up, brushing grass off her jeans and came and sat close to Erin.

"There has to be a logical explanation; these are just coincidences surely." As always, Petra was the sensible one.

"I don't know. I just know something doesn't feel right."

They sat silently for a while thinking their own thoughts.

Petra's parents, just like Erin's, were always busy. Her mum didn't work but she was on all sorts of committees. Her dad worked in Milton as an accountant. Erin's mum, Stella owned a clothes shop, ConSTELLAtions, here in Newton and her dad, Patrick also worked over in Milton. He was in I.T. but Erin was never sure what he did.

"They probably all went to the same business conference together or they went on holiday," suggested Petra.

"Probably," agreed Erin. However, the same old feelings of doubt crawled across her skin, burrowing into her brain, making her question her parents again. Something still didn't feel right, something she'd heard or seen in the past lay dormant at the back of her mind, but she just couldn't bring it to the forefront. The deathly image of her friend swam before her and she suddenly felt sick. Petra didn't seem too bothered about all of this and yet in contrast Erin knew in her heart she had to discover the truth. She decided she wouldn't share her worries. Not yet, anyway.

"Yes, that must be it. Our parents work so hard so we can live in these lovely houses and have wonderful holidays. We can't begrudge them a break occasionally, can we?" Even to Erin, the smile she presented to Petra felt false.

Petra nodded. She was more rational than Erin and would see clarity in something when Erin could only see the problems. "I agree, Erin. Now, you mustn't start imagining crazy things – they are not spying for the government or aliens from another planet." Erin smiled at this, they used to love watching My Parents are Aliens together and conjuring up mad ideas – all of which were completely ridiculous.

"Oh, do you remember when we saw my mum and thought she was an alien?" Petra said. They fell about laughing. With these happy memories shared between them, the mood suddenly changed, the shadows retreated, and the moon shone in the night sky, its kind face watching over them.

"How could I forget!" They were both remembering the time when they had found Petra's mum in a silver suit and huge antennae protruding from her head; they found out later she was trying on a fancy-dress costume. That was after they called 999 and the police had arrived. Petra is right, thought Erin. I mustn't let my imagination go wild. With that thought she decided to make the best of it all.

"Right then, Operation Birthday Party to start immediately," she announced standing and dusting down her hands on her black jeans. She slipped on her Vans and put her hand out to Petra. "Come on you. We have some planning to do."

They walked arm in arm towards the edge of the field planning what they could do for their birthday party, talking of whom they would invite and laughing loudly about nothing, just feeling comfortable being with each other.

Cowering in the darkness, shadows and secrets lay hidden behind them and watched and waited. Their time would come.

Chapter 3

 Z89 woke with the noise of the daily garment drawer clicking open. She didn't want to look; she couldn't cope with another grey. She knew it wouldn't be blue – that was very rare. Please let it be white, she whispered to herself.

Reaching across tentatively she pulled out a white T shirt and white leggings and white underwear. She breathed in deeply as though the air being pumped into her pod was sweet nectar. No experiments today, no pain, no … investigations. She shuddered at the memories of what she'd endured: the constant prodding and poking and measuring; the injections that caused stomach cramps; being left in the dark for 12 hours with nothing to do, nothing to eat or drink. Each time the Orderlies would explain patiently what they were doing. They said it was all to help understand the teenage mind. Whatever it was all about, she had to put up with it.

Z89 quickly showered and dressed. She knew

by the digital clock in the wall she had five minutes until the bell summoned them all for their first meal of the day. Sitting on the bed and sliding her hand into the crack, her fingers searched and found the hidden pencil. She pulled a tiny piece of paper from under the mattress and began to write.

A memory, a sweet memory. Softness and light. My first taste of strawberries and cream. Another memory, of sound. Laughter and joyful voices. When will I hear that again?

She began to fold the paper once, twice … again and again until a tiny paper boat materialised, just like the nice man with kind eyes had shown her. Her memories held tightly into the folds. Without warning the window of her pod clicked and glided to the open position, at the same time, a strident bell rang out. Time to go. Z89 squeezed the tiny boat and pencil, into a crack between the bed and the shower wall, then turned and made her way calmly through the gaping space and down the ladder. She joined the line of girls, most were like herself in white; others, smiling, in blue and a few, looking anxious, in grey. No one spoke, they all knew the consequences.

They walked along a brightly lit corridor to the Nourishment Sector. There they collected their food and then stood behind their stools while the loudspeakers played soothing music. Five boys and five girls stood to attention round each of the tables. A voice broke into the soft cadences of the notes.

"You are one being. You belong here. You are loved."

"We are one being. We belong here. We are loved." The young people spoke monotonously. They repeated it all three times and the music returned. They sat and began to eat.

Two days before her birthday, Erin was in her room listening to music on her phone. She'd asked for a new one for her birthday, hoping to get the new iPhone as this one was on its way out. Erin jabbed her finger on the screen, but Ed Sheeran's voice was disappearing and then the screen went black.

"Brilliant!" she said out loud, flinging the useless phone into a pile of stuffed toys sitting in a corner, waiting to be remembered.

Erin lay back on her bed, staring at the ceiling, gold and silver stars glittering down. Her mum and dad decorated the room last summer. One dark blue wall, Midnight Message it was called in the paint chart, and the other three in a soft Dove Grey. The blue curtains continued the star theme and festooned the ceiling to floor windows that overlooked their garden. There was a small Juliet balcony where she could stand and breathe when life got too much, but Romeo never appeared. She giggled at the thought of Shay climbing up the wall to her balcony. He would probably break his neck. He deserved to!

Shay.

A sudden image of him sitting in her English class speaking the lines of Romeo as her friend, Willow, recited the part of Juliet. Erin of course, was reading the nurse. She never got the glamourous roles. She loved him from afar, watching him eating lunch with his mates, watching him play football on the top playground, watching him cycling home on his BMX. And now, he wasn't talking to her because she'd asked him out and he said he wasn't interested … how embarrassing! What a mess!

A sudden noise came from her soft toys, making her glance across to an enormous grey, plush elephant surrounded by teddies, a wolf cub and various rabbits.

"Okay. Which one of you did that?" Erin asked them, accusingly. Their lifeless eyes stared back at her. Then the wolf cub began to vibrate. "It was you, Xander!" Erin exclaimed, snatching up her phone that was nestled in his paws.

It was working again. Doing anything? Petra had texted. Erin leaned against the elephant and replied.

E: BORED ☹
P: Out shopping with mum. ☺ Want to meet later? x
E: Yes. 7.30 at usual place xxx
P: See you then xxx

Thank goodness for Petra, Erin thought to herself. She keeps me sane. Erin stabbed at the music app seeing as her phone had decided to come back from the dead. But there was nothing. I wonder if Mum has got me that new phone. Everyone is out: Mum and Dad are still at work; Malachi is at his friend's house. I could go and have a look. They're not going to be here for my actual birthday, so what does it matter when I have the phone.

Erin left her room and quickly made her way across the wide landing and climbed the stairs to the top floor to her parents' room. She flicked her long, black hair over her shoulder as she pushed open the door to their split-level suite of rooms, crossed over the slate floor of their open plan en-suite and climbed the glass steps to their sleeping area. Mum wasn't very imaginative when it came to hiding things. Erin smiled remembering her dad finding her one Christmas in the huge walk-in wardrobe surrounded by Christmas paper and playing with her new dolls. He made her wrap them all up again and she had to pretend on Christmas day it was all a surprise just to keep her mum happy.

Becoming a teenager, seemed to make presents smaller and more rectangular, and consequently were much harder to find. She slid open the door to the walk-in wardrobe. Crammed full of designer clothes, shoes displayed on wooden racks, handbags nestled inside cotton bags, various drawers with clear glass fronts so their contents were easily found, the room smelt of her mother's favourite perfume – Chanel Number 5. For a moment that evocative smell made Erin feel guilty about being there in her mum's private space, but then she remembered about the phone. She won't mind, Erin told herself.

Erin began by sifting through the many shoe boxes her mum had stacked. Nothing. Then she opened all the suitcases, packed and ready for their trip away. Still nothing. Damn, she thought. Mum is getting better at hiding stuff. Finally, she pushed her way through the many coats and dresses and found some boxes, all with different patterns covering them, neatly piled up behind several art canvases. They were well hidden under several throws and cushions. Perhaps these were her birthday presents.

Erin sat down on the cream carpeted floor and shoved the canvases to one side. There were three boxes, graduating in size from the top to the bottom. She pulled the top one on to her lap. The box was about 10 cm square, with a swirly pink and blue pattern. She lifted the lid and saw pale pink tissue paper. Erin swallowed - she shouldn't be doing this - but something inside her made her want to look further. She carefully parted the tissue paper. Perhaps Mum had bought her the bracelet she'd seen in the window of Le Ciel Bleu. Nestled in the paper were tiny baby bootees, yellow silk with lacy ribbons. Oh, she thought, lifting them out, these must have been mine, how sweet. Erin stroked the silk tenderly. Mum's kept these all this time. Erin felt a sudden warmth envelop her like a hug. She gently folded them back up again and carefully replaced the lid.

The larger, second box beckoned now. Perhaps there was more stuff from when she was a baby. Erin opened the box, the pattern on the lid was of peacock feathers, vibrant blues and greens. Inside were several smaller boxes and bags. One had a baby's tooth, another contained a lock of blonde hair, yet another held a pink lacy hat and the fourth a miniature silver bracelet; Erin smiled as she encircled two of her fingers with the tiny circlet. These were all hers. How could she have been that small to wear these things? She knew from baby photos and what her parents had told her, that she'd been very small and underweight when she'd been born and her mum had been very poorly for a long while afterwards. Erin carefully placed all the items back in the box and covered them with the lid.

Now for the third box. This one was much bigger and covered in a pattern of brightly coloured butterflies. Erin loved butterflies. Her mind returned to a time when she was about six and Mal was eight and Grandma and Grandad had given them a special butterfly house made of net. They had begun with tiny eggs on the leaves, then they turned into chrysalises and finally they watched the butterflies emerge and perch onto a thin branch Erin had placed inside the net, drying their wings.

The day they let them go was a sad one for Erin, but she knew they had to be free. Living things needed freedom and light, without that they would die. Her father explained it very carefully to her. So, the whole family had gone out to the garden on a summer's day and let the butterflies fly free. It was an extraordinary sight watching them tumbling about in the warm air like colourful snowflakes dancing on air, some landing on flowers, others flying high into the trees and one landing on Erin's outstretched hand. For a moment the butterfly stayed perfectly still, its iridescent wings shining in the sunshine, before taking off and joining the others.

Now, sitting here surrounded by her mother's beautiful designer clothes, Erin opened the box. No tissue paper or tiny boxes this time. Just a cream leather photograph album. The cover held a pattern embossed in silver.

Erin traced her finger over the curling, swirling lines. An M and an E – Malachi and Erin. Her mum loved family photographs and she'd covered the walls of their house with many frames holding their many memories.

Erin gingerly took out the box. Opening the book, she felt a tingling in her fingers. The first page held a picture of Erin sitting on a sheepskin rug, smiling her goofy baby smile. The next a year later as a toddler standing next to a giant book of fairy stories and a rocking horse. Erin didn't remember any of these but she was only young at the time so that didn't surprise her too much, but as she progressed though the album, she found pictures of herself at different ages in places she didn't remember visiting. Rome, Paris, New York; surely, she would have remembered New York, but as the caption said FOUR YEARS OLD, Erin decided she must have forgotten. How could she forget being by the Empire State Building? She would have to ask her parents if they could go back there. As she turned more pages she felt an increasing feeling of apprehension. Here she was in South Africa, there she was smiling at the camera in Japan and yet another of her in Iceland. Erin and her family travelled widely but this was becoming more and more weird. She didn't remember any of this.

Erin finally came to the end. The caption said FOURTEEN YEARS OLD (last year), and there she was standing in front of the Taj Mahal. What the …? When was this taken? Who took the picture? Erin's contemplations were rudely interrupted by a slam of the front door and heavy footsteps on the stairs. She hurriedly returned the album and boxes, piling them up as before and hiding them with the blankets, cushions and canvases.

"Erin!" a deep voice shouted up. "Where are you?" Erin breathed a sigh of relief, it was just her big brother, Mal.

Erin came out of her hiding place and descended the glass steps. As she came down the main stairs, she grinned at seeing her tall, dark-haired brother stretched out on one of the sofas, one leg over the arm and the other trailing on the floor.

"There you are sis." He looked across at her. "What've you been up to? You look as guilty as hell!"

"Nothing. Just chilling, that's all." She flung herself down on to the sofa opposite.

"You've been looking for prezzies haven't you. You've been squidging!" Mal knew her too well.

"I have not!" she stormed back throwing a cushion across at him.

"So why are you blushing?" he threw back at her.

Erin reached for the TV remote and spent some time punching in numbers. The screen jumped from one image to another in quick succession. Nothing she wanted to watch. Turning it off she let out a deep sigh.

"Mal?"

"Yeah." Mal was studying his phone now and grinning inanely at the screen. Probably a picture his stupid friends sent him, Erin thought unkindly.

"Do you remember going to New York?" Erin asked.

"Yeah." He continued to stare at his screen.

Erin sat up straight in the chair. "Really, how old were you? Did I go too?"

Mal looked at her.. "You came with us, but you were only little. Don't you remember going? Why?"

"I don't remember anything. What about Rome, Iceland, Japan?" Erin rattled off various places.

"I don't know why Mum and Dad bother taking you anywhere, Erin. Course we have – don't you remember anything?"

"Well what about the Taj Mahal? We haven't been to India, have we?" This was her trump card.

"We went on that film studio tour and you had a picture taken in front of a mural of the Taj Mahal. Blimey, Erin, get a grip. What is the matter with you?"

Erin stood up. "Nothing."

As she left the room, Mal suddenly called out. "I'm only kidding. We haven't been to Japan or Iceland – I think I would have remembered going there."

Erin felt the ice sliding down her spine again, but this time the cold remained making her shiver.

She turned back and looked at him. "Are you sure?" When he didn't reply, she strode over to him and grabbed his phone.

"Hey, what are you doing?"

"Mal, this is important. I found some pictures of me taken in all of those places we've never been to."

"Yeah right."

"I did."

"Okay so where are these so-called pictures of you?"

Erin sat down on the coffee table and described what she'd found. She told him of the birthday dates too. She could tell he didn't believe her by the way he looked at her.

"What do you think it all means, Mal?"

"I'm sure your imagination is just going crazy, sis. You watch too much rubbish. There will be a perfectly logical explanation for it all." Just like Petra, Mal had a practical head on his shoulders.

"Come and look then, if you don't believe me." Erin stood up purposefully just as the front door opened, and their parents bowled in shouting hellos. She grinned. "I'll show you another time."

Erin continued into the hallway where her dad hugged her, her mother had already disappeared into the kitchen with the bags of shopping. Erin climbed the stairs and looked back at her dad as he hung his green suede jacket in the coat cupboard. He loosened his tie and kicked off his work shoes and started to pad off into the kitchen. Patrick paused and glanced up at Erin. "Hey, princess. What's up?"

"Nothing, Dad." She turned back up the stairs and took them two at a time to reach her room. Once there, she stood at the window. Dad wouldn't lie to me, would he? Should I talk to him as well as Malachi? I don't know what to do. Things were all jumbled up in her head. While pressing her forehead against the cool glass, eyes misting with tears, dark shadows danced around the seven stones in the field beyond. These shadows of the long distant past reflected the images that danced in her mind: photographs of far-away places, forgotten birthdays, baby clothes. Voices drifted through the kaleidoscope of colours and faces: Mal, "We haven't been to Japan or Iceland – I think I would have remembered going there." Her mother, "I love her so much … but it is forbidden. She deserves to know." Her dad, "Why can't you be more like your brother and work hard at school."

Erin sighed, wiping her eyes on her sleeve. I don't know who to trust and I'm sure Mum is lying about something. Taking a deep breath, she came to a decision. The first thing to do is to show Mal those photos. I must try and make sense of all this. I must, or I will go mad!

Chapter 4

 "Z89. Come to the Enrichment Sector, now." An abrupt voice crackled through the sound system and broke into her head like a knife cutting into her thoughts.

She was quietly studying in one of the Learning Labs; reading the play Macbeth by William Shakespeare. They had been reading the text and learning about the Tudor and Jacobean periods of history in lessons; Z89 found it all intriguing. Killing a king seemed rather extreme to her and she was struggling with the language too. Images of Macbeth holding two blood-soaked knives floated before her as she continued to read.

"Z89 Marcon." The crackly voice persisted and a loud cough from behind made her lift her head. Miss Citrine was standing over her waiting for her to stand to attention. Now she became alert.

Z89 closed her book and returned it to the shelf above the desk. A door clicked across and the book was locked behind the glass. She stood and faced Miss Citrine, a short, rather plump woman dressed in daffodil yellow. Her hair was a mass of mousy brown curls topped by a golden ribbon. The colour of her uniform suggested a happy person but, her gaze was joyless and her mouth grim. Beryl Citrine tutted and turned sharply, her saffron heels clicking sternly away; Z89 followed, her own soft shoes silent across the floor.

The Enrichment Sector was different from the other areas in the school. This was where children usually went if they had a blue uniform day. Z89 had been in raptures that morning when a blue uniform appeared in the drawer. She felt an emotion she didn't feel often – happiness.

Further along the corridor a door slid open and they entered. To the right was a long rail holding a variety of clothes; a rainbow of colours in several styles and sizes. Miss Citrine selected a pale lemon dress, dotted with white daisies, short sleeves and a full skirt. She turned to Z89 and gestured to a selection of shoes and pointed to a small cubicle. "Change quickly, my dear." Her voice was sugar, her smile was false.

Z89 realised this was a special day – she didn't know what day or the date – but she'd been in here before and had photographs taken before a giant green screen. She changed into the dress and wiggled her feet into the cream shoes she'd chosen; turning she saw herself in front of the full-length mirror. A selection of wigs lay prone and lifeless on a side table. Z89 chose one, placed it on her shaven head, checked it and then emerged from the cubicle like a butterfly from a chrysalis.

"Very nice," Miss Citrine said coldly. "You will do."

An Orderly in a light brown uniform stood waiting for her, camera and tripod ready. Meekly, her hands clasped together, Z89 sat on a stool and smiled into the camera, she was going to enjoy her hour of enrichment.

Erin stared, unblinking at her phone, while she scooped cereal into her mouth.

"Patrick, that was Mum on the phone. Dad isn't well, so they can't come and look after the kids." Stella, Erin's mum, paced up and down massaging her forehead with one hand.

Patrick Winslow sat at the kitchen table, coffee cup half way to his mouth. He returned it to the tiny gold saucer and sighed deeply. "The kids will be fine – Mal's eighteen and Erin will be fifteen tomorrow. It's about time we made them more independent." He looked across at his daughter who was seemingly absorbed in her phone but was quietly taking in every word of their conversation.

"I know, but I don't like Erin to be on her own for her birthday." Stella suddenly sat and poured herself a black coffee from the pot. The many bracelets adorning her thin wrist clicked against the table as she took her cup and drank.

"She can see Petra as well. It's amazing those two share a birthday and have never celebrated together." Patrick finally took a swig of his coffee. He pushed his glasses back up to the bridge of his nose and absentmindedly stroked his beard, now with a few touches of silver woven into the dark. His tanned face seemed to hide the fact he would be fifty, next birthday. "What do you think, lovely girl?" He poked Erin in the ribs, and she grunted.

"Yeah, that's cool. We'll be fine. Petra and I had already decided to party."

Stella looked shocked. "Oh, I don't know about that. I don't want you drinking or taking anything weird."

Erin stared at her mother and sighed. "We're not stupid. We were going to have a picnic up at the Stones and invite a few friends. That's all."

"The usual suspects, I suppose." Patrick added.

Erin frowned at her dad and returned to her screen.

"Mal can be there to … watch over them." Patrick grinned at his daughter; he knew her better than her mother did. "Give her some credit Stella. They'll have a lovely time without us."

Later, that morning Erin and Mal waved their parents off. The Mercedes purred softly down the road as Stella blew kisses out of the passenger window.

"Right, let's get going," Mal said to his little sister, who looked the true innocent standing beside him. "We have a lot to do."

Mal's little white Fiat was waiting on the drive and unbeknown to their parents they had packed drinks, a picnic, sleeping bags, cushions and their rucksacks. They were on a mission. As they jumped into the car and headed the same way as their parents had gone, Erin thought over the last couple of days and what had led them to deciding to follow their parents to see where they were really going.

The photograph albums had just been the start of it all. Erin couldn't put her finger on what was wrong, but she knew deep in her heart something wasn't right.

It was interesting to see her parents had been away for various birthdays, but Erin eventually put that down to circumstance. Her parents worked hard, and her dad was often away on business. And when Petra had found the same thing had happened to her, again it was weird but could just be chance. But it was finding the boxes hidden away in her mum's wardrobe when Erin began to put two and two together and not even coming up with an answer. She needed to prove to Mal, after he said he'd been winding her up about going to all these countries, that she was rightly suspicious of her parents.

On the same day she discovered the boxes Erin had waited for her parents to go out to their respective fitness classes and then quietly she knocked on Malachi's door. She reminded him of the photos she'd found and asked him to follow her up the stairs to their parents' room and amazingly he had, recognising that his sister was upset about something.

Erin pulled out the boxes and Mal sat looking at the tiny baby things and the photographs. He didn't know what it was all about either. He exclaimed he didn't understand why there was an M and an E intertwined on the album when there were no pictures of him to be found. His suggestion of the letters standing for the pronoun 'me' referring to Erin was met with a loud silence. It was then they hatched a plan to follow their parents to see what was going on. Mal said it was probably a wild goose chase but could see Erin was determined to do something.

Mal and Erin had never been close. They were both so different and Erin often thought Mal was boring – always studying and not having much of a social life. She often wondered if he'd ever had a girlfriend. He worked on Saturdays at a small coffee shop in Newton and when he wasn't doing that or studying, he was playing football. Erin knew he hated being around lots of people and found being enclosed in exam rooms crammed full of sweaty bodies intolerable. There had been a few times, whilst sitting his mock GCSEs, when his anxiety forced him to leave the room, sweat beading across his face, stomach pains doubling him over. Moving him to a small room with just three other students for the main exams made a difference and he'd achieved good grades. He now attended a Sixth Form College in the next town and hoped to go to university.

They collected various items together and packed the car so they could follow their parents to wherever they were going. Mal had bumped into their father in the hallway; Mal was carrying out sleeping bags.

"It's just for a sleepover, Dad," he explained.

"Well as long as you are not away while we're away. I'm trusting you to look after your sister."

"You can trust me, Dad." Mal grinned, knowing full well what they were planning. Earlier, he'd suggested to Erin they should just ask their parents, but she was adamant that idea wouldn't work.

Now, sitting in Mal's pride and joy, his little white Fiat, Erin looked across at her brother. "Thank you," she said.

"What for?" Mal asked.

"For doing this for me."

"That's okay. I know you're a bit mad sometimes, but you've got me thinking."

"I'm sure there's nothing going on. Hey, at least we can surprise Mum and Dad on my birthday!"

"True," agreed Mal. "This will certainly be a surprise for them."

They could see their dad's dark blue Mercedes up ahead; two cars in between. Their dad indicated to turn onto the motorway and Mal followed staying behind another car; he'd just passed his test, and this was the first time on a motorway for him.

"Erin, keep them in sight. We have to stay back so they won't see us."

Erin watched as the powerful Mercedes sidestepped smoothly into the fast lane. "You're going to have to speed up, Mal, you know Dad likes to drive fast." His knuckles were tightening on the steering wheel and his face took on a determined expression. "You can do this. I trust you," she encouraged.

Erin had tried to get Petra to come along with them, but Petra said she thought Erin was completely nuts and that she needed to stay at home to look after her younger brother. Erin promised to keep in touch and let her know what they found out, if anything, but Petra said quite vehemently she didn't want to know. She and Erin had parted on bad terms and Erin was disappointed in her friend's attitude towards her. What was Petra scared of? she thought now as she helped herself to a toffee from a bag in the glove compartment. She unwrapped another and passed it to Mal, who took it without taking his eyes from the road ahead. He sighed, and it seemed to Erin he was beginning to relax into his driving.

They travelled south for several hours along motorways and soon realised they were heading for Cornwall. Once they were off the motorway, it was much harder to remain hidden from their parents. There had been a few times when they felt they were getting too close to the Mercedes ahead of them, but they had been lucky when another car pulled out from a side road and then a tractor came between them. It slowed them down, but by this time they began to recognise where they were. Erin joked Mal should be in a car chase in a movie where the good guy is following the bad guy. At this, he pulled a face that clearly said, never again!

Welcome to Castleton, announced a large brightly coloured sign, as they approached a charming town with skinny side streets and a smattering of shops. They knew this area quite well from previous visits to a splash of a village nestling on the North coast a few miles away. Erin hoped they were going to stop soon. She'd been feeding Mal sandwiches while he drove, but he was getting tired and they were both thankful when their dad indicated right to turn into the car park of a place called The Three Towers, a four-star hotel. They pulled over to the side of the road and Erin hopped out, crossed the road, dodging cars as she ran to the high wall surrounding the hotel. Peering round the gate post, she waited until she saw their mum and dad enter the reception and then waved a signal at Mal. He pulled in and parked the car in a shady spot out of sight at the back of the building.

Erin followed the little Fiat and waited while Mal turned off the engine and then stretched. "Now what do we do?" Mal said opening the door, unfolding himself and clambering out.

"We'll have to sleep in the car." Dusk was falling and Erin rubbed her hands to keep warm.

"I'm starving," Mal said. "I saw a burger place back along the road. I'll go, I need to stretch my legs. You stay here and see if you can find out anything."

Erin agreed and gave him her order: a large coffee, chicken burger and fries. She realised she was hungry too. She quickly texted Petra—Erin would keep her side of the bargain and keep her informed, whether she wanted the information or not and then climbed out of the car. Having recognised the town of Castleton, while driving along its narrow streets twisting and turning underneath the remains of a castle high on a hill, Erin remembered it had not been a happy experience the last time they visited.

Locking the car, she zipped up her jacket against the cold breeze that was threatening to grow into a fully-fledged wind. Inside her jacket nestled the blue brooch her parents had given her that morning as an early birthday present – it was a butterfly with the words *Fly high and free* engraved upon it. Erin made her way across the car park and round to the front of the red brick building to the reception to see what might be going on, but the receptionist wasn't much help. There was no business convention going on and no there wasn't any training for business owners and no she couldn't tell Erin where Mr and Mrs Winslow were at this moment.

Erin returned to the car, having purloined a local map and some leaflets from the receptionist. They were only about twenty miles from the sea here and were just over the border into Cornwall. The castle that overlooked the town was, according to the leaflet, "begun after the Norman Conquest". Erin was fascinated by history and would have loved to visit the crumbling round tower, but not this time.

A loud knock on the window made her jump. Then she saw Mal's grinning face above steaming cups and large paper bags full of food. She leaned across to open the car door for him to climb in.

"Anything?" he asked.

"Nothing," Erin answered. "There's no conference here," she added as she took the food he offered her.

The next morning, they were woken by a dawn chorus of songbirds. It was early and still dark, but a line of pink etched out the horizon, like a highlighter on a sentence, and as the sun rose the castle beyond was clothed in a warm glow.

It had been an uncomfortable night, Mal squeezing his tall frame into the back seat of the tiny car while Erin stayed in the passenger seat. It was cold too. Erin finally slept only to have strange dreams of her mum and dad living in a huge castle perched on a cliff. The waves smashed against the jagged rocks below and lightning flashed. Erin could see them standing there on an ornate stone balcony, but she couldn't reach them. She tried to stagger across a long thin bridge that separated her and them, but the force of the wind and rain pushed her back. The rain mingled with her tears as she stood feeling desolate and abandoned. Then soft music came to her in her dream – it was insistent, getting louder and Erin struggled into wakefulness - it was her phone alarm. She dozed and then found herself being shaken by strong arms. Rubbing her eyes and stretching like a cat, Erin asked, "What time is it?"

"Just gone 7. Happy birthday, Erin." He grinned at her, his dark hair standing up in spikes. He passed her a box wrapped in brightly coloured paper; it was the bracelet she'd wanted from her favourite shop in their little town.

"Thanks, Mal."

She could feel tears prick her eyes as she enclosed her wrist with the strands of thin grey leather held together by a silver heart. "And thanks for doing this for me." Awkwardly, she hugged her older brother.

Later, after coffee and doughnuts collected by Mal, they felt a bit more human. They took it in turns to sidle into the hotel and use the loo and have a quick wash and teeth clean. Erin waited for Mal, by the car, scrolling through birthday messages from family and friends and a brief message from Petra. An officious-looking man in a black, security guard uniform suddenly came into view and stalked over to Erin.

"This is private property, Miss. Are you staying in the hotel? I don't seem to have your registration number on my list."

"Oh yes. We're just checking out, thank you." Erin smiled at him, hoping he would leave them alone. "We arrived late last night and didn't have time to register our vehicle."

At that moment, Mal came running across the car park. "We need to get going. Mum and Dad are leaving ..." He tailed off as he saw the security guard and skidded to a halt. Erin could see he was trying to be nonchalant towards the situation, but she soon realised he wasn't very good at pretending. "Hi. We've just arrived to collect our parents," he explained as he sauntered across to them. "Is there a problem?"

"That's interesting, *Sir*. This young lady said you had just checked out. Which is it?"

Erin and Mal both started speaking at once. The man held up his hand and they paused mid-sentence.

"That's enough. I don't have you registered which means you are trespassing. If you don't leave immediately, I will be calling the police."

Apologising profusely, Mal climbed into the car, telling Erin he'd seen their parents and turned on the engine. Nothing happened. The engine stayed obstinately silent. The security guard began to tap on his phone. Mal swore under his breath and tried again, still nothing. The guard was lifting his phone to his ear when Mal tried again and this time the car roared into life. They managed to drive away just in time, as Stella and Patrick Winslow came out on the main steps. Erin caught a glimpse of her parents dressed as though they were going to a wedding – a dark blue suit for Patrick and a bright red woollen coat over a grey dress for Stella.

Mal parked the car around the corner where they could get a good view. A few minutes later, their parents' car appeared at the main gates, turned left and purred past them.

Following at a distance and staying well back, after about half an hour of snaking along country roads, with high banks either side and few passing places, they saw their parents' car turn into a wooded area, where a dusty lane led them to a car park. They held back until Stella and Patrick parked. Other cars passed them finding parking spaces and then disgorging their passengers all dressed to the nines.

Mal pulled over under the shadow of a huge ancient oak tree, its branches stretching out as if to protect the car. Erin was the first to extricate herself. Mal soon emerged and looked around him. They glimpsed a stone building through a wooded area and started to walk along a path that wound through the trees and bushes, but abruptly stopped when they saw in front of the open doors, of what seemed to be a stately home, two armed guards checking their parents' bags and papers. The guards gestured to Stella and Patrick to enter and then they disappeared from view. As they watched, the other people from the car park began to arrive. Each time they were checked thoroughly before going inside the building.

It was a beautiful house, Erin observed, symmetrical with big Georgian windows filling high walls. Semi-circular steps led up to the enormous double doors of dark wood; one stood open to allow guests to enter. In front was a sweeping drive of gravel that curled around the house like an elegant necklace. Evergreen shrubs of dark green, shaped into spheres were growing within an ornamental garden to the left of the house. Stone sculptures of goddesses were placed at intervals to add interest. The cold wintery sun was now higher in the slate grey sky and tried to throw some rays down on to the garden to give it some warmth. Tiny green shoots were thrusting their heads hopefully out of the dark loamy soil, some already had nodding yellow flowers turning towards the sunshine. It was March 1st, a Sunday. My birthday, Erin thought to herself as she drank in all that she saw.

The two guards in black suits and dark glasses were now patrolling the front of the house. No one else entered and it seemed everyone they were expecting had arrived. One of the guards checked a sheet on a clip board, nodded at his colleague and they retraced their steps, returning to the main doors. They too disappeared, and the door was closed behind them.

"We'll have to try another entrance. Let's try the back," Mal whispered.

They returned, back through the trees and skirted round until they came to another path, more overgrown than the other one, and slowly and silently made their way towards the right side of the building. Here they found a single white door, with ornamental trees in large gold pots either side, but on turning the handle discovered it was locked. They continued round the back and came into a small courtyard where they could see a flurry of movement, there were waiters and waitresses collecting boxes, crates, trays from the back of a red truck and taking them into what looked like a kitchen area.

"Wait here!" Erin instructed Mal and before he could protest, she hurried to the truck and started carrying a box of glasses. She hoped to blend in with the others as they were all dressed in black just as she was.

As she walked towards an open doorway, she quickly glanced across to where Mal stood watching her from the safety of the trees. He was hugging her coat she'd thrown on the ground before dashing off. Even from here she could see he was tense. Erin couldn't believe it – she was taking over, and her big brother couldn't do a thing but watch and wait.

A thin, bald man with a long scar on his right cheek, approached her as she went to enter the building. "Where's your ID?" he asked sharply.

Erin smiled and spoke to him calmly. "It's in my inside pocket," she lied. "I'll get it out as soon as I can take this heavy box in."

The man nodded, unsmiling and gestured for her to enter the kitchen.

This is easy, she thought to herself. Now, all I've got to do is find Mum and Dad and see what they are up to.

Chapter 5

 "Z89, be quick." Another of her teachers stood at the door and beckoned her over. She was quite petite and looked like she should be a nice kind person as she had dimples, a round face and happy eyes, but Z89 knew differently. Never trust Professor Amber Hessonite. She could turn on you like a wolf fighting to protect her cubs - she wouldn't protect you; she would feed you to the wolves.

"What must you remember?"

"We are one being. We belong here. We are loved." Z89 replied, looking straight ahead.

"You must only say good things about the school. You must not touch anyone or allow yourself to be touched. You must not accept any gifts." Z89 nodded.

"Miss Hessonite?" Z89 spoke quietly.

The round-faced woman narrowed her eyes as Z89 stood patiently waiting. She was dressed in a yellow and white dress, with her tiny feet pressed inside white leather heeled shoes with a bow sitting on the top. Her long, black hair was tied back with a white silk ribbon.

"Refer to me with my full title. Professor …" The teacher emphasised this with a gleam in her eyes. "… Hessonite."

The young girl was horror stricken she'd forgotten the teacher's title and began to stammer. "S s s sorry, Professor Hessonite. I forgot my manners." She looked at the woman in front of her, who was wearing a long jacket in apricot over a fiery orange straight dress and an amber necklace and earrings. Her flat, comfortable shoes in tangerine completed the look. "Where am I going?" Z89 asked tentatively.

"You will find out soon enough."

They left the Green Room and with Professor Hessonite walking quickly, Z89 found herself scurrying along to keep up. Stumbling occasionally in the unfamiliar shoes, she was used to wearing the flat soft shoes of everyday, the girl felt uncomfortable, her dress bulky and stiff as she moved. The two of them soon arrived at the lift doors where they found the rest of Marcon – four girls and five boys – waiting patiently for the doors to open. Three teachers stood to the side of the group as though they didn't want to be contaminated by these young people. No one spoke. This was normal. But one of the boys looked momentarily at Z89. He did not smile, but she noticed that he slowly brought his thumb and forefinger of his right hand together as he went to scratch the side of his head. She thought the shape he made looked just like the shape of a tear.

The lift doors opened, and the teachers ushered them into the awaiting metal boxes which swallowed them up like a whale consuming plankton. The doors closed, and the lifts ascended.

"In here," said a man dressed in a black tail jacket pointing to the kitchen and handing her a pristine, white apron.

Erin walked past him trying to look confident, but inside butterflies were flying around madly in the pit of her stomach. The head waiter accepted her statement that she was another waitress sent by the agency and was late because of being held up in traffic. He was obviously short staffed and getting quite anxious about serving all the people in the restaurant.

One of the chefs, sweat dripping from his forehead, suddenly shouted at her to take some plates to table 10 in the restaurant. Erin carried them through the swing doors and looked around her. The room was very ornate, with crystal chandeliers flashing sparkles of light from above. There were ten circular tables, each one covered with a snowy-white table cloth and at each table sat two adults and one child. Erin was mesmerised by the tranquil scene around her just for a moment and assumed the groups of three were different families; they were all talking calmly and quietly together. Her eyes searched the room for Patrick and Stella, but couldn't see them.

Weaving her way through the diners, Erin glanced from side to side at the clear numbers placed in the centre of each table. Everyone was dressed in beautiful vibrant colours as though it was a party and yet there was no communication between the tables, no balloons or presents. Erin finally saw number 10 near the long thin windows and made her way carrying the tray of steaming hot food to the group of three sitting there. She stopped abruptly, almost spilling the roast dinners and tiny gravy boats that sat squarely on her tray. It was Petra and her parents. Her best friend had lied to her. Erin couldn't believe it. Couldn't get away, she said. Petra had made out her parents were going to be away just like Erin's, and she would have to stay at home and look after her brother. Yet, here she was about to enjoy roast beef and Yorkshire pudding.

As Erin placed the plates in front of the three people she stared pointedly at Petra, but the girl ignored her. "How could you?" Erin said through gritted teeth, but the girl looked through her as though she didn't exist.

Petra's mum looked up at that moment as Erin, dressed as a waitress stood before her. Her eyes widened with recognition and then she hurriedly made a small gesture with her hand, gently lifting her fore finger to her lips as though to keep Erin silent. She was suddenly aware of a man in dark green standing near them; he seemed to be listening to their exchange and took a step towards Erin. "Move along there," he ordered sternly.

Erin turned away and started walking back towards the kitchen. Her thoughts were whizzing wildly round her head like fireflies in the night. What is going on? Why did Petra ignore me?

People were all eating now, and the conversation was a little more broken. Erin made her way carefully round the tables but stopped as she heard familiar voices to her right. Stella and Patrick were sitting at one of the tables. Her father was tucking into his dinner. His favourite, Erin thought to herself, absentmindedly, and then realised a young girl was sitting at the same table with her back to Erin. She had a similar build to Erin but much thinner. She was wearing a yellow and white dress she herself wouldn't be seen dead in and her long black hair was tied back into a neat pony tail.

Erin didn't want her parents to see her there, but she had to see who was wearing that awful dress. She skirted around behind an ornate trifold screen and a display of huge ferns and exotic flowers, that hid the entrance to the kitchen. Hiding behind the screen, Erin peered through a gap towards the table where her parents were sitting with this stranger. Erin gasped and held her fist against her mouth to stop herself from crying out. The girl sitting there looked exactly like Erin. Black hair scraped back from a thin face, her skin as white as porcelain. Her smoky grey eyes looked intelligent and she rested her pointed elfin chin gently on her long thin fingers, as she listened to Patrick describing a car he'd seen and wanted to buy. It was a mannerism that Erin also had, and she watched transfixed as a girl, who could only be described as her twin, smiled at a joke Erin's dad had made.

Erin stared at the little group. Stella passed the girl a tiny present wrapped in silver paper with a blue bow sitting on the top. "Happy birthday, Miranda. We love you. Don't ever forget that."

The girl pushed a tendril of hair, that escaped the tight hair style, behind her ear and reached across to take the present. As she opened it, Erin saw the girl smile. She placed it by the side of her plate. "Thank you, but I can't accept gifts." Stella wiped her eyes with her napkin and sniffed quietly.

"But, it's your birthday, surely they will let you. I will speak to someone."

"No, no please don't make a fuss," Miranda, the girl said quietly. "Please don't." The look she gave to Stella silenced her and then she sniffed again.

Patrick, who had been fiddling with a small piece of paper, suddenly passed it over to the girl. "Hide it in your shoe. Pretend you have dropped something," he whispered. Miranda gently covered the paper with her hand and with her other hand knocked her knife onto the floor. She bent quickly to retrieve the knife and as she did, she deftly slipped the tiny folded paper inside her shoe. She sat up breathing deeply and looked around her. Erin watched the girl's face closely, taking in the strain shown in the lines in her forehead, the white skin that had no make-up and the sadness in her slate grey eyes.

"Thank you," she whispered to Patrick.

At this Patrick spoke in a louder voice. "You are looking well, my dear. How are your studies going? Are you working hard?" Erin, still hiding behind the screen, smiled at this. Typical dad questions, she thought to herself.

Erin looked across the room, to where Petra was sitting and at that same moment the girl looked up and their eyes met. There was no recognition in the other girl's eyes, no warmth, just an ice-cold stare. Erin felt a shiver and knew this girl wasn't Petra. She hurriedly scanned the faces of the other people around her but didn't see anyone else she knew. Who were these people? Where had they come from? She had questions buzzing round her head and felt quite dizzy with what she'd seen.

A rough hand suddenly grabbed her arm and spun her around. It was the head waiter. "You, missy. What do you think you are doing? You are paid to work not waste time hiding. Get back in the kitchen!" he stormed, pushing her towards the swing doors, where another waitress was coming through with an armful of hot dishes.

"Sorry." Erin twisted away just in time to then fall against another person who was carrying a tray of glasses. They side stepped around each other like ballroom dancers doing the tango and amazingly nothing was dropped. Erin hurried on through the kitchen and out into the courtyard. She could see Mal standing where she left him and ran to him falling into his arms, breathing heavily as though she had run a marathon.

"We've got to go," she stuttered.

"What happened in there? What's going on?" Mal frowned at his sister.

"I'll explain in the car," she shouted running towards the car park. "Come on, we must go!"

A few minutes later, they were back in the little Fiat. Erin took a long drink of water from the half empty bottle she'd squashed into the door pocket. Wiping her mouth with the back of her hand she announced, "I have a twin sister."

"What? You can't have, I would know if you did. I remember Mum and Dad bringing you home from hospital and there was only one of you." Mal laughed but stopped when he saw the look on Erin's face.

Erin described what happened in the restaurant and more importantly, who she'd seen.

"Did anyone see you? Did Mum and Dad see

you?" He buried his head in his hands. "God, what a mess."

"I think we should find out where this girl lives. She must live somewhere near here." Erin pulled the map out of the glove compartment.

"What about this girl who looks like Petra? That's really weird." Mal had always liked his sister's friend and was struggling to take all this in as well as trying to stay calm.

"Yeah, I know. It was definitely her parents because her mum saw me."

Mal finally came to a decision. "Right then. We'll wait to see if they drive away somewhere and then we'll follow them."

"What do we do about Mum and Dad?" asked Erin.

"We'll visit them at their hotel later. I think we need to ask a few questions."

They waited and it was some while later before they saw movement up ahead of them. A convoy of three black cars made their way stealthily to the main gate. The windows were all opaque; Mal and Erin were blind to who was inside.

"What do you think?" Mal asked.

At that moment, the first car came to a standstill at the main gate, the side window opened, and something was tossed out onto the grass beyond. The car then purred away turning right onto the main road, swiftly followed by the other two.

"Let's go!" shouted Erin suddenly but as the car arrived at the gate, she asked Mal to stop. She hopped quickly out of the car and then climbed back in.

She had in her hand a tiny silver box. She saw her parents give this to Miranda. She carefully placed it in the glove compartment and looked out through the gloom of the early evening to the headlights ahead of them.

They drove for endless miles, Erin's heart racing unlike the car. She leaned forward willing the Fiat on. I want to see her. I want to talk to her. I want to know her. Erin chewed her ragged nails as her thoughts whirled around her just like her butterflies when she was a child. Ahead of them the three cars indicated right and turned off the main road and up a narrow lane. They could see their lights following each other until the cars stopped and the lights were extinguished.

Mal drove on to the grass verge and they both climbed out, grabbing coats and making their way along the narrow road. Grass grew down the middle and potholes full of rainwater pitted the tarmac. Up ahead they could see a farmhouse to the left and a couple of farm buildings on the right, but that was it. The road ended there and there was no sign of the three black cars. Mal shone his torch around the area, but there was nothing.

"I don't understand this," he said. "Those cars definitely came down here."

They retraced their steps back to the main road. It was as though the three cars never existed. Erin shivered and pulled her coat around her. "We could ask at the farmhouse."

She started back up the lane before Mal could reply; he followed her, casting his torch over the grass verges. No tyre tracks, no sign of life, nothing. Erin walked along the garden path. The light above the front door shone out like a beacon, illuminating the garden where daffodils were pushing up green shoots. The lawn to the left of the path was neatly trimmed and the vegetable patch to the right was regimented and tidy. She stopped at the small porch and lifted the woodpecker shaped knocker. Its beak rapped its message on the oak door but there was silence from within. Erin turned away to exclaim to Mal and then a light went on inside the house and the door opened a crack.

"Who's there?" asked a thin voice, and then a small pink face appeared with brassy blonde hair above and a smiling mouth with scarlet lips.

"Hello. I'm sorry to bother you, but we're lost. We're trying to get to Castleton." Erin had already thought about what she was going to say. "Does this road go anywhere?"

"Who's that, love?" another voice, much deeper and rounder than that of the woman. A large bear of a man appeared and smiled at Erin through a thick black beard. "Lost, you say? What are you doing out here on the moor at this time of night, lass?"

Mal now joined Erin on the doorstep and continued to explain they must have taken a wrong turn. He said they had seen other cars come up this road and thought this would lead them to where they wanted to go.

The man's face cracked into an enormous grin at that. His weather-beaten face was kind, his dark brown eyes sparkled. "No," he said. "You must be mistaken. No cars have been down here tonight my lad. Go back to the main road and you can carry on until you get to Thorpe Cross, then take a left and follow the signs from there." At that, he closed the door and Mal and Erin were left on the doorstep.

"Let's go and find Mum and Dad," Mal said. "They can help us hopefully."

They turned and retraced their steps, pausing momentarily to search the area in front of the farmhouse and its neighbouring buildings, but there was nothing. They walked back up the lane to the car, but if they had stopped and looked back, they would have seen a light come on in an upstairs room and the man they had met, speaking frantically into a mobile phone. He was angry as he shouted down the phone and watched the two young people walk away; his free hand tightening into an angular fist.

Erin and Mal were unaware of how their visit

affected the occupants of the house as they climbed into the little car and made their way back to Castleton and to their parents.

Chapter 6

 Z89 removed the dress and shoes quickly, scratching her shaven head. The black wig that now lay lifeless on the chair in front of her made her head feel hot and sweaty. Carefully removing the scrap of paper Patrick had given her, from inside her left shoe, she saw it had been folded into a tiny paper boat, just like the ones he'd given her twice before. She could make out words neatly written enfolded into the paper sails. Z89 dressed herself in the white uniform of shapeless shirt and leggings and hid the miniature boat inside the waistband; she would read it once she was back in her Nod Pod.

Opening the door, she saw the nine other Marcon students come out of their respective cubicles adjacent to the Green Room and they all walked in line along the sterile white corridors. They passed another queue of ten waiting to go into a Learning Lab, no one speaking, no one looking right or left. Friendships were not tolerated. This was all part of the programme. She smiled at one, a tall slim boy who was very aware of his height and who held himself slightly bowed, his shaved head beginning to show ginger tufts. He smiled back and made no comment, and then he went to scratch his head, but he did it with his thumb and forefinger pressed together to make a teardrop shape. He was in Febcon, and often wore grey just like her. She carried his smile within her as she walked on; it warmed her heart that someone responded to her.

The ten Marcon students split into two groups, the girls turning off the main corridor to their Nod Pods as the boys continued to theirs, at the opposite end of the school. Z89 went to climb her ladder, she was exhausted, it had been a long day.

"Hello, Z89." The sweet, sickly voice came from behind and Z89 whirled round to face the purple creation that was Esme Dorling, the school Principal. "How was your Enrichment experience today, my dear?"

"Very nice, thank you, Miss Dorling." Z89 was polite and calm on the outside, but inside her stomach was rolling back and forth like the waves on the sea she'd only seen in pictures. She didn't want the paper boat, hidden in her waist band, to be found and set forth on to a sea of destruction.

"I understand you accepted a gift." Miss Dorling's voice was like liquid toffee but had a brittle quality. "Where is it?" The voice changed, and the face changed like a chameleon coming out of its camouflage, and her true being was clear to everyone. She put out her hand, like a lizard stretching out its tongue for a fly.

"Someone took it from me. I didn't keep it. They threw it out of the car, Miss Dorling." Z89 swallowed hard. "I never opened it," she finished lamely. Esme Dorling gestured with pointed fingers as though to acquiesce but then grasped Z89's arm with contempt. The pain was instant, the purple pointed nails dug in deeply and her muscle was twisted sharply.

"I'm watching you." The proud, skinny woman breathed into Z89's face, her eyes glinting from the stark white light overhead, her stale breath flowing into the young girl's nostrils. Then, she was gone, her dagger heels clicking away along the corridor. Z89 realised she was holding her breath and slowly exhaled, her heart pounding. She took a deep breath and climbed the ladder to the side of her, until she reached her Nod Pod; there she lay on her bed, tears scratching at her eyes.

Looking up at the low ceiling, Z89's silent tears slipped down into her hairline. Closing her eyes an image of a man, who makes paper boats, and a woman, who smiles with her mouth but shows true sadness in her blue eyes, merged with the tears. She'd seen them before but didn't know who they were. They said they loved her, whatever love is, she thought to herself. Yet, she felt a warmth wash over her whenever she saw them, engulfing her like waves of the sea.

She pulled out the paper boat, carefully unfolded it and began to read the message wrapped inside the folds.

 The door to the hotel room opened softly and Stella Winslow peered out, blinking at the hotel manager who stood before her.

"Yes, what do you want?" She was abrupt, then frowning hard she wrapped her thick towelling dressing gown tightly round her thin body. Her eyes red and swollen, her face looking old in the pale light, Erin noted as she looked at her mother. The manager explained they had two visitors and asked politely if they were happy for them to visit. Before Stella could reply Erin pushed past the hotel manager and barged into the room with an apologetic Mal following. She flung herself down into one of the comfy armchairs and waited for her mother to respond. Stella waved the blue suited man away and nodded her agreement, assuring him they were her children.

"But we're not your only children are we, Mum?" Erin fired at her harassed mother who looked stricken at seeing her daughter and son. "Who is she then? Where does she live? Why have you kept her hidden all these years?" The quick-fire questions Erin shot out, hit her mother like bullets. Stella almost physically tried to dodge the sharp words and when Patrick entered the sitting-room she ran to him for protection. He held her in his arms, and she erupted into more sobs.

"Come on love," he soothed and led her to the small sofa. "Mal, why don't you put the kettle on lad? I'm sure we could all do with a cup of tea."

Erin sat fuming, drumming her fingers on the arm rest while her brother took control and made tea with a calmness that annoyed her intensely. The only sound was the ticking of a clock and an occasional sob from Stella. Mal handed round cups of strong tea and then perched himself on the armrest next to Erin. That small gesture settled her, she realised he was on her side and together they could find out what was going on.

Mal opened the discussion, laying his hand gently onto Erin's arm. "Erin says she saw you both with a girl that looks just like her. We didn't come here to upset you, but we feel we're owed some sort of an explanation."

Erin sipped her tea and nodded, afraid of what she might say. She didn't want her mum to be so upset but she was very confused and suddenly felt very worried; tears pricked her eyes and exhaustion washed over her.

The clock ticked away the seconds and yet to Erin it was more like hours before her father answered.

Patrick finally replied, still holding onto Stella's hands tightly. He looked at his wife searchingly and she nodded. "That was your twin sister, Erin. Her name is Miranda."

At that Erin let out a little sob, Mal put his arm around her giving her a protective cloak to hide behind. She knew this must be true because of what she'd seen, but to now hear the truth from her dad, her lovely dad who she trusted more than anyone, she could feel her world spiralling out of control. Erin gasped for breath like someone drowning in deep water, she coughed and then emerging from her place of safety she slowly stood and stumbled to her parents. She fell into their arms and they held her tight. "I don't understand. Why did you keep this from me?"

"We had to. No one knows. No one must ever know." Stella finally found her voice. "I'm so sorry you had to find out like this. We have been so careful." She looked panic stricken at Patrick. "What if they find out?"

"If who finds out?" Malachi asked. "What will happen? Look, why are you both being so secretive? You're beginning to worry me."

"Please," Erin implored. "Just tell us about Miranda."

The air thickened around Erin as she waited for more lies from her parents. She didn't really want to know about this strange girl who looked like her but conversely, she was desperate to fit the pieces of the puzzle together.

"I don't know about you lot, but I need something stronger than tea." Patrick made his way to the mini bar and pulled out various miniature bottles, he found four glasses and placed everything on the coffee table between them. He broke open a bottle of white wine and passed it to Stella, who was now sitting with Erin at her feet. He helped himself to a whisky, gulping a large mouthful down before speaking.

"When Mal was born, we were broke. We lived in a tiny bedsit in Milton above a hair salon. I still remember the smell of the bleaching fluid permeating the flat." Patrick took another large mouthful of the amber coloured liquid and savoured it for a moment. "We had set up a business but lost everything and were bankrupt. I began a job in I.T., but it was as a trainee and getting paid a pittance and then your mum became very depressed."

Stella looked sorrowfully at her children. "Post-natal depression. It was awful."

"Anyway, a friend told us about a scheme that could help people like us who were struggling financially." Patrick looked across at Stella for support.

"Yes, that's right." Stella looked wistfully into her wine and swirled it around the glass. "Then I became pregnant again and when I learned I was expecting twins we realised we had to do something as we couldn't feed one child, never mind three. So, we … we …" she tailed off.

"What did you do, Mum?" Erin looked at her mother with a pained expression. "Dad? Please tell us," she implored. "No more lies."

The clock on the wall counted the empty seconds, beating a rhythm as regular as a heartbeat. For Erin, time stood still at that moment. She felt as though she was standing on a precipice not sure whether to jump into the unknown or to go back to the past. One thing she was sure about was that after today, her life had changed for ever; she had to plunge on and find out the painful truth.

Patrick sat down wearily and rubbed his hand through his greying beard. "You have to understand there was nothing else we could do." He paused. "Your mum was so poorly, and it was very distressing for everyone. Anyway, we went along to a special meeting where we were told they would set us up in great jobs, they would find us a beautiful house, good education for all our children on one condition."

"What condition, Dad?" asked Mal.

Stella took a deep breath, leaned forward and whispered. "The one condition was that one of the twins would be educated away from home and we could only see her once every five years until she was eighteen and then she could come home."

Erin gasped. "I don't understand."

Patrick continued explaining, taking sips of

whisky like full stops at the end of each sentence. "They decided Miranda was the one to go away. It could so easily have been you, Erin." At this Erin looked uneasily at her parents. "They came to the hospital, did lots of tests and took lots of measurements on you both and then took Miranda away. We didn't see her again until her first birthday. We have regular updates on how she is, we're sent pictures of all the places she has visited, and they allow us to see her once every five years, like today. Miranda seems very happy at her school and the education she receives is superb; a very bright girl by all accounts."

"The photo album, Erin!" exclaimed Mal. "You're not going mad. The pictures were of Miranda."

Stella stared at Mal in amazement. "You've seen them? How? When?"

Erin explained about looking for birthday presents and coming upon the pictures. Stella put her head in her hands and began to rock back and forth. Patrick patted her shoulder, trying to calm her. Glancing at his watch he suddenly exclaimed, "Goodness. It's way past midnight." Patrick swallowed the final drop of his whisky. He looked drained, Erin thought.

"Now, I think it's time to get some sleep," Patrick continued. "It's been a very long day and we're all exhausted. We can talk again in the morning. Miranda is fine and settled with her life. Don't worry, guys."

Erin jumped up, knocking,the glasses and tiny bottles flying. "So that's alright then is it? Your explanation for hiding her all these years, all these lies you keep on telling us – that's made it all okay now." Erin stood breathing heavily. "You sold my sister to …" she searched her mind for the words, "… someone and you don't even know who they are. Just so that you could have a nice life with your nice shop and your nice friends. You make me sick. You could have managed somehow." Her voice was rising as her emotions began to take over. "How do you know she's happy? How do you know she's well cared for? You hardly ever see her." Erin was shouting now. "She is part of me." She clutched her fist to her heart. "I always knew that part of me was missing. I always felt there was something not right with me and how you treated me. I need her. You might not, but I do." Erin grabbed her jacket and made for the door, pulling it open sharply. "How could you do this?" Her final question hovered in the air as she ran out and disappeared down the dimly lit hallway.

As Erin stood silently waiting for the lift, Mal arrived, still looking shaken. "I told them we would see them in the morning," he said and as soon as the doors slid open, they almost fell in.

Once they were back in the car, they both relaxed. "What do you want to do?" Mal looked across at Erin, who suddenly seemed unsure of the next step.

"I don't know. I just had to get out of there to think. I can't take it all in."

"Nor me. I never knew, you know; I haven't lied to you like they have."

Mal looked far into the darkness as though he seemed to be remembering distant memories. "I remember the strong smell of bleach when I was little, and it often made me feel sick. Mum was always crying too; I never knew she was ill. I used to think it was because I was very naughty."

"The bleach smell would have been the chemicals they used in the hair salon, below your flat."

Mal paused and then sighed deeply. "That's not the first time I've heard the name Miranda." Mal looked across at Erin, who was now staring sharply at him.

"What do you mean?"

"I remember Mum talking to Aunt Angela. They were arguing about something and Mum was really upset. Angela said Miranda was happy and in the right place. I didn't think anything of it at the time, I just assumed they were talking about a friend of theirs." Malachi dropped his head and then mumbled. "Sorry, Erin. That's all I remember."

Erin glanced at him and realised he was exhausted. Her big, strong brother was silently crying. "I've lost a sister too," he sniffed and wiped his hand across his face. Erin rubbed his shoulder for comfort and passed him a scrunched tissue she found in her pocket.

"I think we should try and get some sleep. It will all look better in the morning," Erin whispered, not really believing that.

They pulled out their sleeping bags and pillows and each tried to get comfortable. Erin tossed and turned until finally falling into a deep sleep where dreams took her to a strange farmhouse where she was put in a cage and her parents ran off laughing with a girl that looked just like her.

Chapter 7

"Z89. You are being punished for accepting a gift. Today, you will face various challenges. These will help us with our research into the human mind and body. Your suffering may help other young people have a better life." The voice came clearly over the spherical white speaker in the corner of the white room. Z89 thought it quite ironic that the Correction Sector was bright white which represented purity of heart and why they wore white on a normal day. Here she stood now in the grey uniform of someone who was to be looked down on, to be abused for bad thoughts or actions. She thought the room ought to be grey and dull too. Colours were very important here at Zephyr.

"You will enter the Garden of Perception where nothing is as it seems. Here you will stay for one hour and you will report on your experience."

A door slid open and Z89 could see a small paved area. The sun was shining down on lush green plants and trees. She was puzzled - how could this be a punishment? Stepping through the door, which slid silently back into place behind her, she could hear birdsong and the trickle of water. She wandered towards these delicate sounds. As the trees thinned out, the girl could just make out hundreds of thin ragged shapes hanging from rails high above her. She pushed her way through the jungle of greasy rags, coughing at the overpowering smell of oil. They clung to her like limpets on a rock and she battled to get through.

A broad lawn stretched before her and she breathed deeply, clearing her nostrils and throat. She stumbled; the ground was shifting, its uneven surface causing her to lose her footing several times. A cobbled path led into a sloped area with several tall round pillars standing in a circle; Z89 counted seven in total. On the top of each pillar plants grew in abundance, some with twisting leaves spilling over, others with spiky fingers clawing towards the sky. She strained to see what was growing there and reached out to lean against a pillar. Touching what looked like smooth stone, she winced as sharp thorns drove into her soft palms.

Z89 began to feel quite disorientated as the pillars were vertical and then appeared to be leaning. The regular square stone slabs she stood on in her bare feet seemed to tip and turn and soften until they turned to dense green grass. Nothing was what it appeared to be; her perceptions of reality began to twist and change in her mind.

Gentle music began to play, softly to begin with, and the young girl began to relax and breathe deeply. Sitting on the cool green quilt of grass, enjoying the lyrical violin and piano playing in the background, she found herself becoming sleepy. Z89 relaxed. At the same time as her eyes closing, discordant notes jarred the air, and the beautiful music became ugly and oppressive, becoming louder and louder until she had to cover her ears to block it out. The ground suddenly tipped up and she found herself rolling and rolling, down and down until she hit a huge rock jutting its head out of the ground. A tranquil pool of water lay beyond and Z89 could make out small silver fish darting around under the surface. The music stopped, abruptly.

A yellow smoke sleepily snaked its way across the lagoon but Z89 couldn't escape - she had to breathe it in. Surprisingly, the aroma was sweet, and she found the tension in her shoulders dissipating. It reminded her of almonds and ginger, of vanilla and cherries. She breathed again, deeply this time and struggled to her feet. Staggering into the yellow haze, the slim girl found herself being smothered with sweetness. Not an unpleasant experience, she thought. The taste on her tongue was of caramel and chocolate, but then without warning the smoke changed to a luminous vitriolic green. The stench of rotting flesh, of decomposing food and of human excrement overpowered her senses. She bent over, coughing, bile coming up unbidden and spilling out onto the cobblestones around her feet. Z89 dropped to the ground, suddenly dizzy and light headed; the putrid fog poured over her skinny body.

The next few days dragged on; Erin returned to school and her studies. Everything she learnt about her family whirled around her head and she found herself daydreaming when she should be concentrating in her lessons. Her mum contacted the school on the Monday morning from the hotel and explained that due to family circumstances Erin wouldn't be in school until Tuesday 3rd March. Her parents had driven her back home; the silence between them all was deafening. Mal drove back separately promising he would come straight home; he didn't have any lessons at college on a Monday.

Erin sat in her room contemplating history homework and thought over what had happened.

Once they arrived home, her dad took her quietly into the living room and sat her down. He explained again patiently why they sent Miranda away. Erin felt cheated, let down by him. He was the one person she'd always gone to for help.

When her mum was getting at her he would give her a hug and suggest calmly she should allow her mum some space as she had a very stressful life running a business and looking after her family. Now sitting there surrounded by family photos and expensive works of art, and as her father explained again their reasons, Erin began to understand some of the pressures her parents had been under and the guilt they lived with every day.

"Why couldn't you tell us? Why did you feel that we wouldn't want to know?" Erin still wasn't satisfied with her dad's explanation.

Patrick stroked his beard thoughtfully. He tried to explain to Erin what he'd gone through, how he felt so useless at times, that he couldn't save both of his beloved daughters. He told her that as Erin had grown older, he battled with his decision all those years ago, but he knew there was nothing they could have done. In fact, he realised quite early on it hadn't been his decision to make. He finished by saying, "There were some very influential people involved in the decision making, and in the end, we were forced to hand over our tiny baby."

As her father had been speaking, his eyes filled with tears. "You just have to take my word that we had no choice." Patrick turned to his daughter and took both her hands in his. "Do you trust me, Erin?"

Erin looked at her father. He looked tired and

old. "Yes, Dad, I do."

"Then we must just keep on going. We will see Miranda when she is eighteen. We cannot see her or talk about her. You must not tell anyone what you have seen. Until then, you have to work hard at school and try not to have detentions." He laughed at her sad face. "Chin up, lovely girl." He held her tightly.

Erin was silent for a few moments thinking about everything he had told her. Then she said, "Where does Miranda live? Is she at a boarding school or does she live with another family?"

"She is at a boarding school, but we're not allowed to know where it is. It's to stop families from contacting their children. I assume it's near the place we saw her."

Erin was astounded. "Don't you care where she is?"

At this, Patrick jumped up and said with some force, "Of course, I do! Don't start telling me how I should feel about giving away my daughter. You must remember we're not in charge here. If we do anything wrong, it could affect our whole family. We agreed all those years ago and now we face the consequences."

Erin was shocked by her dad's outburst but there was still something gnawing away in her mind. "What about Petra? I saw her parents there with her twin. What do I tell her? She has a right to know."

Patrick said vehemently, "No. You must not tell her. We would get into serious trouble with the authorities."

Now, Erin sat in her bedroom, staring out of the window, thinking of her dad and all the things he said and how he had reacted. Nothing makes sense, she thought. Finally, she turned to look at her text book and pulled it towards her; World War Two – not a time in history I like, she thought to herself. The Holocaust was the title at the top of the page, and she read the first paragraph making neat notes in her exercise book, finding it heavy going. However, once she began to read, she found it fascinating and soon half an hour had flown by.

The waves of nausea came slowly to begin with, then her stomach became knotted and twisted. These weren't butterflies in there – these were elephants stamping around in hob nail boots. Erin stood to go to the bathroom, but the dizziness brought her crashing back down, she could feel bile coming up and held her hand to her mouth. Again, she staggered to her feet and just made the bathroom in time.

Later that evening Erin began to feel better. Her mother had found her draped over the toilet, horrified at the state of her daughter, and immediately helped her into bed. She fussed around her just like she had when Erin was a little girl. She told Erin she was obviously exhausted by everything that had happened and brought her a tray with her favourite food, ham and pineapple pizza, all carefully cut into bite-sized squares. Erin found she was starving and soon tucked into the hot food.

There was a knock at her door and Mal's smiling face appeared. "Can I come in?"

Erin grinned. He never usually asked. He would always just barge in and throw himself on to her sofa and grab the TV remote, but this evening he came in and quietly sat on the edge of the bed. "How are you feeling?" He looked worried and Erin smiled again.

"I'm okay. Why is everyone being so nice to me?"

"We care about you, that's all." Erin looked surprised and then he reached over and tousled her hair grabbing the remote before she could object. Helping himself to some pizza, he grabbed a cushion and pulled himself up to sit next to her. Erin relaxed. Thank goodness, he's his normal self, she thought.

She hadn't seen much of him since he returned from Cornwall. The last few days had been busy with school and college for each of them respectively. The evenings taken up with karate classes for Erin, football and rugby training for Mal. This was the first time they had been together, just the two of them, since discovering Miranda.

"Did you?" Erin suddenly asked as Mal flicked

through the TV channels.

"Did I what?" he asked back settling on some comedy programme on Dave.

She dug him sharply in the ribs. "You know what. Did you go back to the farmhouse?"

"Of course, I did. But there wasn't much to see."

Erin grabbed the remote from him and pressed mute. "Tell me. Did you see her, you know, Miranda?"

Mal finished eating the piece of pizza and then began to describe what he'd seen. After seeing his parents and sister off he retraced their steps from the night before. He walked back up the lane but this time he went looking around the barns. They were full of bales of straw, tractors and ploughs. There was nothing strange about the farm buildings apart from the CCTV cameras that were dotted around the place. He had hidden at the side of one of the buildings being careful not to be seen. He told her that as he'd stood there, it suddenly dawned on him how spotlessly clean the farmyard was – shining white concrete, no mess, no straw, nothing. It was far too clean for a busy farm.

Erin stretched her legs, she was getting cramp in her toes, but she quickly settled to take in what Mal was telling her. It was at least an hour, he said, before anything happened. He almost gave up but then a huge door in the building next to the farmhouse slid open and a sleek black car emerged. It purred through the farmyard and stopped outside the gate to the farmhouse. A man dressed head to toe in brown, his face hidden by a hood, climbed out of the driver's seat and pulled open the back door of the car.

At that point Mal stopped and stared into space. Erin shook his arm to make him continue. He looked up. "I watched the front door opening and out stepped a woman. She was purple. She looked quite formidable, like a headmistress."

Erin stared at him. "What do you mean she was purple?"

"Purple hat, dress, shoes."

Mal described how the woman walked down the pathway with some purpose. Once she was in the car, the driver climbed back in and drove off down the lane.

"Is that it?" Erin demanded feeling frustrated she hadn't been there.

"That was it. The only thing that struck me as strange was it wasn't the woman we met the day before. She could have been visiting them I suppose. It just looked odd – the car appearing out of the barn like that and the farmer and his wife stood at the door, both were crying, and the purple woman had a face like thunder."

They sat quietly for a moment. "Perhaps they had an argument," Erin suggested. "I'm sure they have nothing to do with Miranda." But we did see those black cars go up that lane, she said to herself, and Miranda, our sister, was in one of those.

Where did they all go?

"Ah, well. I might be able to shed some light on that," Mal answered mysteriously.

"Really! What did you see?"

Mal helped himself to more pizza and explained he'd left the farm and driven back to a nearby petrol station as he was running on vapour. He parked the car after he filled up with petrol and went and got himself a coffee and doughnut at the little café that stood next door.

Erin was beginning to get impatient but tried to wait and see what he was building up to. "Anyway," he went on. "I sat down at an empty table and began drinking my coffee."

Mal had been aware of a girl who entered the café and sat at an adjacent table. He described her quickly to Erin. She had spiky white blonde hair with pink streaks, dark eyebrows and piercing blue eyes. Several gold rings were coiled round her tiny earlobes and she wore a scarlet leather jacket with Bring Me the Horizon, carved into the back. At this point in the very detailed description, Erin looked at Mal, and it slowly dawned on her this girl had made quite an impact on her brother.

"Okay, so you fancied her. What has this got to do with Miranda?"

Mal blushed. "No, I don't. Cara was …"

"Oh, Cara is it? When did you get her name, brother dear?"

He went on to describe how he and Cara started

chatting and she introduced herself. He very politely asked her to join him and they started talking about Cornwall. She asked him where he lived and what was he doing here in this god-forsaken place – her words, he said. He hadn't been sure whether to mention the farm they visited, but as the conversation went on and after another coffee, he relaxed and told her everything that had happened to them.

"You what?" Erin was incredulous. "This is a secret. No one must know."

"Who says?" he retaliated.

"Dad says."

"Yes, but Cara knows this place. She knows all about the farm. She can help us."

"Really? Tell me then." Erin laughed. "I know, they are aliens, beamed down from Mars."

Mal paused and then looking directly into his little sister's eyes. "There is a school there. But it's hidden from view. The school lies beneath ground level and the farmhouse is the main reception area. Miranda is in that school." Erin looked at him open mouthed. What was he saying?

Chapter 8

 Z89 sat quietly watching the others. There was so much she wanted to say, but she must wait her turn. Everyone in the circle wore white except for the teacher who was in green; everyone had shaved heads except the teacher who had short grey hair; everyone was different - the colour of their eyes, their skin, the shape of their nose and mouth, and their voices, when allowed to speak, ranged from gruff and deep to high and sweet.

Z89 enjoyed the Communicate sessions. They could speak freely, if they followed the statement they were to discuss.

"Z77, what are your views?" The grey teacher turned to a red-faced boy sitting to his right.

The young man rubbed his face and blinked hard several times. "Sorry. My views? On what?"

Mr Verde leaned towards him and poked him with his silver topped walking stick. "Wake up boy. Men are stronger than women. What do you think?"

The boy blinked again. "I think … I think women are very strong. They have to go through hours of pain and discomfort in childbirth."

The girls nodded. They had all seen the film recording and all silently decided they were never having children.

A deep voice came from the other side of the circle. "Men have to be strong as well. It's their baby too. They have to be very brave when they have to give their baby away." It was Z42 Febcon who had spoken. Z89 looked at the young man sitting opposite her, his long legs stretched out in front of him and crossed at the ankle. She thought he looked very relaxed. She could see there were still tufts of red hair pushing through his scalp and automatically scratched her own shaven head, feeling a few odd tufts beginning to grow there. Their eyes caught, just for a moment and she hurriedly looked down as she clasped her hands tightly in her lap and began to study the short nails on her right hand.

Mr Verde smiled. "You are quite right, Z42. That is part of the life cycle of humans; babies must be taken away at birth, so parents cannot prejudice them while they are growing up. Children should not be like their parents; they should make their own choices in life."

Erin found herself sitting at the front of her English class, right under the long nose and sharp eyes of Mrs Hamilton. There was no escape from her glare and now, Erin found herself becoming very uncomfortable.

"Come on, Erin. We haven't got all day. Read out the passage. Thank you." The teacher spoke in a short snappy way, expecting everyone to do her bidding.

Erin coughed and then began to read from Animal Farm. Once she started, she became more fluent and quite enjoyed reading it out loud, until she was hit on the back by a hard object and she stuttered to a standstill.

"Now what?" Mrs Hamilton had been following the story and not seen Erin being hit by a large furry pencil case, as it turned out. Erin held up the bright pink weapon.

"Someone just hit me with this, Miss."

"Honestly, year 10. What am I going to do with you? Who threw it?"

The heavy silence in the bright, airy classroom spoke no words but was punctuated by commas of laughter. A deep voice came suddenly from behind Erin. "It was me Miss. Sorry Erin. I was trying to hit Digby." The laughter bubbled up and then exploded as the boy, Alan, stood and grabbed the pencil case, catching Digby by the shoulder as he returned to his seat. Digby reacted by gesturing a finger at the others.

"That's enough class. Quiet down now." But the students had had enough of learning. It was a Friday afternoon, only half an hour to go until the bell and freedom. Digby reached over and pushed a pile of books off Alan's desk.

Mrs Hamilton decided to change tack. "Right you two boys, detention after school. The rest of you can answer the questions on the sheet about chapter 3." When she saw other pupils smirking at this, she added, "And anyone who doesn't complete the work may be joining them."

Erin waited for Petra by the school gates. It wasn't like her to be late, she thought. She checked the time on her phone for about the tenth time and decided to give up and make her own way back. Erin hoisted the heavy school bag onto her shoulder and turned towards home. Thankfully it wasn't far. The school was half way up the hill, a large red brick building sitting in state, an imposing edifice for the new children who began there, but as time went on it became more of a home for some and a prison for others. Erin always felt trapped at school, but she loved to draw and found she could escape to the art room to find solace. One more year here and then freedom, she thought to herself.

At the top of the hill instead of going straight home she carried on towards the Place of the Seven Spirits. Here she dropped her bag on the altar stone and rummaged through books, PE kit and various chocolate bar wrappers until she found her sketch book and pencil. Sitting with her back against the cold stone, Erin opened the book and flicked through her last few sketches. Since coming back from Cornwall, she hadn't been able to draw. Every time she tried, the pencil strokes seemed to have a mind of their own and she would become frustrated and finish up scratching sharp lines through the images.

Now, her pencil began sketching what she remembered about the farm in Cornwall. Soon, she had a rough outline of the house, and a bird's-eye view of the farm buildings mapped out in front of her. She recalled what Malachi told her and thought to herself, this is mad. We're in the 21st century – why would a school be hidden underground? There must be a logical explanation. She still felt very uneasy about everything that had happened and wished she could talk to Petra - she's the practical one, she'll make sense of it all.

Throwing the sketch pad onto the ground, she pulled her knees up and wrapped her arms around them, hugging herself. Sitting there, looking out across the chocolate box market town, contemplating her frustrating life, Erin was suddenly aware she wasn't alone. A voice she recognised came floating across the grass. It was Petra – finally - she thought. As Erin began to scramble up, eager to see her friend, another voice joined the first, a deeper, richer sound punctuated by soft lilting laughter from Petra. Her best friend was with someone, and Erin knew exactly who she was with. Erin grabbed her bag and sketch book and crawled behind the altar stone. She didn't want to be seen, but she wanted to see why Petra had brought Shay to their special place.

The two voices, one soft, one warm, came closer until Erin could make out the words.

"I don't know, what do you think?" Petra was saying.

"I think it's a good idea, Pet." Erin was astonished. Her friend didn't allow anyone to call her that. She watched from behind the cold stone as they both sat down with their backs against one of the Spirit rocks. To Erin they seemed to be getting rather too close to each other. Shay's black dreadlocks fell across his face and he brushed them away as he bent towards Petra.

"Should we tell her?" It was Shay asking a question.

"No not yet. We need to get used to the idea, now we've finally found each other." Petra turned towards the boy who Erin had loved from afar for so long. Then, to her consternation, her best friend who knew how Erin felt about Shay, flung her arms around the boy of her dreams and they held each other close. Erin backed away to hide further from her friends and cried silent tears. She slunk away quietly, not wanting to hear any more of their conversation.

"Oss." Erin bowed respectfully to her karate teacher, her Sensei. She felt empowered when she was in her white Gi, the thick cotton jacket and trousers, with the black silk belt wrapped around her tiny waist.

The class began, Erin standing at the left-hand side of the training room with the other black belts, the rest of the students lined up alongside, their belts creating a rainbow that stretched to the other side of the room. Working her way through the different colours, over the last few years, meant that people showed her respect by bowing to her. Each grading was challenging, but nothing more so than that final grading. She had just turned fourteen and been quite intimidated by the many men and ladies who were already black belts, watching her, testing her, sizing her up. But, she did it and they were impressed by her technique and her spirit. Now, standing here, Erin used her karate to calm herself after the earlier encounter at the Spirits. She wanted to punch and kick until the pain and anguish of being let down by her friends, her family, even Mal who seemed besotted by this girl, Cara, would evaporate and she could be the girl she was before, and life could return to normal.

Erin moved through the series of actions that made up the kata she knew so well, feeling a sense of peace. Her body remembered the strong, powerful movements and the slow gentle gestures; they were part of her soul. Erin bowed at the end and realised what she must now do. One of the morals learned by practising karate was to defend the paths of truth. She wanted to find out the truth behind Petra and Shay; the truth behind her parents, but most of all the truth about Miranda. She needed to meet her, to know her and to be part of her life, whatever it cost.

The weeks seemed to fly by. Erin met with her friends and Petra was often there, but now there was a barrier between them. Neither of them knew how to break it down. Willow and Elsa were good friends, yet they didn't understand Erin like Petra did. Erin began to spend more time with Nadir; he made her laugh and that was what she craved. They started meeting at the Seven Spirits. Nadir practised Kung Fu and they shared martial arts moves. They usually finished up laughing at each other especially when Nadir did a voiceover impersonating a sports commentator.

One evening they were standing in the centre of the seven rocks, facing each other, bowing with respect, when Petra and Willow appeared.

"Hi guys," called Willow. Her make-up, as usual, was impeccable, although Erin knew it wasn't just worn for effect. Scar tissue from when she'd been burnt quite badly, as a child, by a scalding kettle, smothered one side of her face. She had pulled the cord dangling over the kitchen worktop and that was it. Erin was amazed by how her friend never complained and just embraced life in every way.

Now, Willow came over to them with Petra trailing behind her. Nadir and Erin broke off from sparring and mumbled a hello.

"Hello, Erin," Petra said pointedly. "How are you?"

Erin shuffled her feet, put her hands in her pockets and sighed. "Good, thanks. You?"

"Yeah, good."

It was Nadir who broke the awkward silence that followed. "Right ladies, what will it be?" He grabbed his rucksack and after scrabbling around for something, he produced, like a magician pulling a rabbit out of a hat, several bars of chocolate, some crisps and bottles of coke and lemonade.

Willow grabbed the largest bar of chocolate – she had a very sweet tooth. Planting herself on a rock and ripping open the foil wrapping she announced, "Thanks Nadir. We're not just friends with you because you can get stuff for free from your uncle's shop, you know. But it's nice for you to share them with us."

"There has to be some perks to the job," Nadir replied, twisting off a cap on the coke. It fizzed furiously and spurted over his shirt. He wiped the droplets away with his hand. Nadir worked for his uncle at weekends, carrying stock, cleaning the floors, serving customers – and he always had food and drink in his bag.

Erin and Petra took some crisps each and sat down not talking.

"What is it with you two?" asked Willow.

"Nothing," muttered Erin.

"I don't really know," Petra said suddenly standing. "It's ever since you went away, you just won't talk to me." She stood facing Erin. "Please tell me what I've done wrong."

Erin looked up at her friend. I can't tell you, she thought and out loud she said, "There's nothing wrong." In her mind's eye she saw a sudden image of Petra kissing Shay. She stood and then, grabbing her bag and coat, Erin made her way through the long grass to the entrance, throwing words behind her. "I have to go … sorry … it's getting late … can't stop."

"Hey, wait!" shouted Nadir. "What's the matter?"

"Nothing. Nothing's the matter. I must go home, my grandparents are coming over." With that Erin turned away and hurried towards her house on the corner.

She could feel their eyes boring into the back of her skull. Why couldn't she talk to Petra? What was stopping her from sharing what she knew? I hate secrets and lying to people, Erin thought angrily, arriving at the driveway to her house. Passing a bright red sports car in front of the house, she smiled; her grandad loved to drive fast and they were here early as usual.

What she said was true – her grandparents were coming over that evening. Turning the key in the lock, Erin wasn't surprised when the door was pulled open and there stood her grandad. Marcus Trent was a formidable character, 75 years old but still very upright and athletic. "Erin, my favourite granddaughter!" he exclaimed.

"Your only granddaughter!" replied Erin snuggling into his warm embrace. Saying this made her think of Miranda. How did her sister feel about her absent family?

"There are two of us," she whispered into his thick jumper.

"What's that? What did you say? My hearing is going a bit. Getting old, I suppose." Her grandad sighed.

"Never mind. Nothing important. How are you, Grandpops?" She stepped back, closed the door behind her and studied his face closely. His brown eyes twinkled below bushy grey eyebrows, his skin reddened raw by cold winds and the hot sun from hours walking his two beloved dogs – two chocolate Labradors – Fizz and Pop.

They strolled arm in arm through to the kitchen, while Marcus shared with her what he'd been up to in their little cottage in Norfolk. He was always making something in his shed or repairing various battered old appliances.

Erin could see her grandmother, Dinah, sitting in the big armchair that looked out to the garden. She was drinking tea and looked relaxed. Her silver-grey hair was cut short and contrasted well with the red woollen dress she wore with a vibrant purple and scarlet scarf.

Kneeling on the floor, next to this elegant woman, Erin smiled up at Dinah's life-worn face. The grey eyes crinkled as she smiled back and leaned over to hug the thin young girl. Dinah stroked her granddaughter's long black hair and remarked how well she was looking.

Later that evening, Erin gently knocked on her brother's door. His gruff voice replied, and she entered. Since Mal had met Cara, he seemed more distant. The brother and sister had never been close, Erin often felt her parents loved him more than her. But, during their time in Cornwall Erin felt closer to Malachi. He was on her side for a change and she felt his equal in them both not knowing about their sister, Miranda.

Mal was sitting on his leather gaming chair, staring at his phone and hurriedly pushing in a message. His school books were piled around him and a text book lay open on his lap. "Yes?" he said without looking up from his screen. "I'm busy. Revising. I have an exam tomorrow."

"Yes, I can see you're revising," Erin laughed. "Revising your new girlfriend." She sat down on the black leather bean bag that was slumped next to his desk. "Can we talk? About Miranda."

Mal looked up at that. "I didn't think you wanted to. I thought you were going to carry on as before, just like Dad suggested."

"Tonight, spending time with family got me thinking about our sister. She should be part of this, getting to know her family, not stuck away where no one cares about her."

"We don't know she's unhappy. It's the only life she's known so she has nothing to compare it with."

"Yet, sitting there knowing Mum and Dad have lied to us, I began to think about what else they haven't told us. I don't know what to think or do any more. I don't know who to trust or who to listen to. I just feel hollow inside."

"I know what you mean. I feel it too."

"I do know we have to meet her. Miranda, that is. I want her to be part of our lives now." Erin then tried to explain how she felt throughout her life of there being something missing. "I have had pains and aches in my body, but the doctor can never find anything wrong. I have been ill for no reason whatsoever. Sometimes I have a voice speaking to me in my head, telling me things and there is this feeling that part of my heart is missing." Erin looked up at Mal. "I've never told anyone this, not even Mum and Dad."

"Then let's go and find her," Mal encouraged. "Cara can help us."

"Do you really think you can trust her, Mal?"

"Yes, I think so. Anyway, she is all we have who knows anything about the place where Miranda is incarcerated. We have to try, don't we?"

"Alright. We need to have a plan this time though. We break up for Easter this Friday, 27th March. I have got stuff on at the weekend, but we could go down on the Monday or Tuesday."

"What are we going to tell Mum and Dad?" Mal looked worried.

"I've already thought about this. We'll tell them we're going camping in Wales with friends. They won't know where we are when we contact them through our phones."

Mal and Erin talked late into the night, deciding what to take with them, what they were going to do and what else they needed to know before going. Cara texted Mal about the school, there was a lot of security and it was extremely difficult to get in without the proper papers. Strangely , she seemed to know how to help them. Mal trusted her, so Erin had to as well, even though when Erin went to bed that night, she had an awful twisted pain in the pit of her stomach. She was scared this might not end well.

Erin slept at intervals but was jolted awake again and again as dreams of being caged up and hearing the key turning in a rusty lock smothered her. In her head she could hear Petra and Shay laughing as they embraced. Her mother and father holding the hands of another girl and then a green fog that twisted and turned around her ankles rose up like a tiger and roared in her face. In the distance she could see butterflies, hundreds of them of every colour and then she saw all those who loved her, pulling off their wings. Erin watched as the tiny lifeless bodies fell to the floor of the cell. She scooped them up and sobbed. She would never be free. A distant crash of thunder pulled her awake and she slid out of bed, padded to the window and watched the storm rolling around the coal black sky. Pulling a blanket from the bed, Erin covered herself against the cold of the night, curling up to her giant teddy for warmth and finally slept.

Chapter 9

 Z89 lifted her face towards the sun and breathed in deeply. The air tasted fresh and clean. This was her time to feel free, even if it was just for one hour. The bench where she sat, was hard and unforgiving. She ignored the discomfort enjoying the rich blue sky above her. White wisps added to the picture and the occasional bird brought song to her ears. Z89 was suddenly aware of someone sitting down at the end of her bench. She looked without turning her head and was pleased to see it was Z42. They sat in silence.

"Get up and walk." The voice echoed around the lush green parkland. "Orientation is your time for exercise."

The young man and girl stood up together and began to stroll along the many paths that zigzagged around the area. They fell easily into step with each other.

"You may talk." The voice came again, and gradually like a stream babbling and then turning into a rapid river all around them came voices, words, phrases, laughter. The blues, greys and whites around them joined one another in twos, threes and fours. Z89 smiled and listened for a moment before speaking to the tall thin boy who walked beside her.

"How are you?" she asked politely.

"I am well, thank you."

Z89 now noticed he walked with a slight limp. "What happened to your leg?"

"Oh, nothing, just another experiment." He stopped and turned to her. "I like you," he said. "Can we walk together again?"

"I like you too. Yes, we could meet on the bench." Z89's heart was beating fast at the thought that someone liked her, but anxious this might get her into trouble.

As though he read her thoughts he said, "We must be careful though. We have to be seen talking to others too." At that, Z42 gently touched her hand. It was momentary, but it was like an electrical impulse. She'd felt that before and then it caused her pain, but this was different. The boy stepped away and as he lowered his arm Z89 saw him deliberately putting the tip of his forefinger against the tip of his thumb. A teardrop shape.

Abruptly, he turned away and walked towards a group of three boys who were standing talking quietly under some trees.

Z89 looked around. She had to talk to

someone. Z63 walked past with another girl deep in conversation. Z89 fell into step with them and joined in.

Driving down a high banked narrow lane, they could see the camp site beyond with a few colourful tents in a row; a dog was barking at some children playing football and a flag was flapping in the strong breeze coming in from the Atlantic. The weather was changing – it had become warmer over the last few days, but today's wind made it feel a lot colder. On the far horizon, the cobalt blue sky met the pale blue of the sea and the patchwork quilt of fields stretched out over rolling hills.

Cara was standing by a wooden gate, the entrance to the campsite, waiting for them. She was all in black and her white blonde hair contrasted with the darkness. She stood with confidence, her shoulders back, her feet astride and her hands thrust into the pockets of the leather biker jacket. A gleaming red motor bike stood proudly at the side of the road, a matching helmet sitting on the scarlet leather seat. Erin felt slightly nervous at meeting the older girl. Erin had never been confident apart from when doing karate and now any confidence she did have evaporated and was plucked by the fierce wind that blew around them.

"Hi. You must be Erin." Cara reached out to shake hands. Erin put her hand out gingerly and a warm slim hand took it.

"Hi," she mumbled.

Mal hugged the stranger and his eyes lit up as she hugged him back. "Good to see you, Cara."

"This is your home for the next few days." Cara waved her arm towards the campsite beyond the gate. "Not my idea of comfort though." She suddenly laughed out loud; perfect white teeth appearing from behind her crimson coloured lips.

While Mal and Erin unpacked their tent and set up camp, Cara put a kettle on to the small gas stove they brought with them. Later they sat around hugging their mugs of coffee, there was a chill in the air and Erin threw on her fleece. Mal passed her a chocolate bar which she devoured gratefully. Lunch seemed a long time ago. They would have to find a supermarket soon.

Almost as though she read Erin's mind, Cara said, "There is a small supermarket in the next town. Do you want me to come with you to show you where it is?"

Mal nodded and Erin decided she would stay at the site while the others went off being hunter-gatherers. She didn't want to be 'a gooseberry' as her dad would say. She waved them off and then sat down to text her dad to tell them they had arrived. There were three texts from Petra, which she'd previously chosen to ignore, but now with four hundred odd miles between them she decided to take a look.

'You okay? Not seen you. Can we meet?'

Then …

'I need to see you. Shay and I have a secret to share.'

Of course, you have, thought Erin. I saw you together. I know your secret.

The third was more mysterious. 'Shay says he knows. He needs to warn you.'

Erin pondered these messages for a few moments and then deleted them. The last one stayed with her though – what did he need to warn her about? Probably, just to stay away from him and Petra.

"Hey. Can we come in?" Mal's voice came as a welcome diversion from her thoughts.

She looked up to see her big brother standing with armfuls of shopping. "Come on you, stop looking at that screen. It will make you turn blue!"

"You can talk." She laughed at the silly phrase their mum always said to them. "You must be positively purple by now!"

She helped him empty the bags of food and they stored them carefully in the small fridge and plastic boxes they brought with them. They were both chatting away, comfortable again with each other, now they were finally doing something that might give them some answers. Mal deftly threw a loaf of bread, then apples across to Erin, who caught them and put them away. It began to feel like the camping holidays they had with Mum and Dad, when they were younger.

"Hi," Cara's voice broke into the fun. She was carrying a sleeping bag and pillow and a small rucksack.

Erin stared at her, she felt betrayed. So, this was Mal's plan, for him and his girlfriend to get cosy together. "Hi." She muttered as she backed away to allow Cara to enter the tent. It was quite a large tent, with an area at the front for relaxing and eating and curtained off sections at the back for sleeping, but now with three of them standing there looking awkwardly at each other, it seemed quite confined.

Cara grinned sheepishly. "I just thought it made sense, you know, with me sleeping here. Then I don't have to keep coming back and forth from home."

"Where is your home?" Erin asked pointedly.

"I live in Castleton, with my dad." Mal grabbed Cara's stuff and stowed it away in one of the sleeping sections.

They were only about five miles from Castleton, and Erin couldn't see that short distance being too much of a problem for a girl with a lovely shiny motorbike, but decided she had to let it go.

"Can we go over to the school now please,

Mal?" Erin looked across at her brother who nodded slowly.

"I think we need to take this carefully, Erin," Cara announced, sitting down firmly on one of the camp chairs. She crossed her long slim, denim clad legs and stared at Erin with piercing blue eyes. She wasn't ready to go anywhere.

Erin could feel herself getting frustrated, she seemed to have no control over the matter. She couldn't get to the school by herself being so dependent on the others. Erin still wasn't sure about this girl, this young woman who sat before her. She wanted answers now.

"Alright," Erin said stiffly, sitting down opposite Cara. "Perhaps it's time you tell me what you know." The words came out like sharp stones being thrown at a window, but they fell short and Cara just smiled.

"You don't trust me, do you, Erin?"

Erin shuffled in her chair, took a deep breath and looked directly at her opponent. She looks like the Ice Queen, thought Erin, with her spiky white thorns for hair, so sharp with gel that even the crash helmet couldn't dent them; eyes as cold as steel and her sharp, angular features. She decided she would pretend to trust her. Her instincts were warning her to take care.

"Erin?" Mal asked. He was still standing near the sleeping sections but now came over to his sister. She felt very vulnerable at that moment, but as her brother stared at her she steeled herself, raising her chin just like she did when she was about to spar with someone in karate.

"Erin?" he said again.

"Yes, Cara. I trust you, because Mal trusts you." Mal sighed at Erin's reply.

"Good. I am glad. We have enough enemies to contend with without us not being a team." Cara reached down to pick up a black folder. "I'm sure you have some questions. What would you like to know?"

Erin and Mal began to bombard her with questions, some of which she answered, others she skirted round. How do you know? What is this place? How can we see our sister? Is it dangerous?

Finally, the brother and sister stopped, exhausted by the exchange and trying to absorb the information she had presented them. Cara had photographs of the farm and the land surrounding it, but little else in her folder. One thing she did have she saved to the end. The piece of yellowing paper she passed to Mal was old and wrinkled.

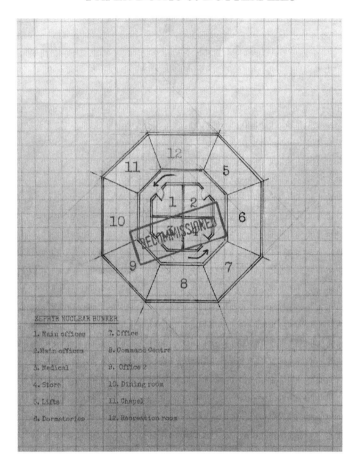

"I don't understand," Mal said passing the paper to Erin. "This isn't a school."

Erin studied the paper carefully, turning it over, but finding nothing on the reverse. The faint lines that cut into the aging thin skin of paper showed an octagonal pattern with smaller octagons radiating from a central square. Each of the shapes had a series of connecting lines; some labelled, others left blank. In the bottom left hand corner, the words, Zephyr Nuclear Bunker could just be made out. One word had been stamped across the whole map -Decommissioned.

She handed the paper back to Cara, who then held it up grinning.

"It is the school! The school is underground within the secret nuclear bunker, completely hidden from view. No one can get in and no one comes out, unless they have permission. The farm is the reception area. The bunker lies directly beneath the farm and the surrounding fields." Cara took the paper back. "This is a plan from 1946, when it was first built after the Second World War. It was withdrawn from use in 1970."

Mal was intrigued. "Really, that's amazing. I've heard of underground bunkers from wartime. Dad and I found a website about one." He paused and thought for a moment. "Okay, so we know a bit more about the place, but …"

Erin cut in, "… what we want to know is, how do you know all this if it's such a secret.

What is your connection?"

Cara's eyes narrowed. "My father has done some research over the years. He found the plan in an old notebook given to him by a friend who passed away."

"But, how do you know this is below the ground?" Mal asked.

"A lot of this is guesswork, unfortunately we can't be sure. That's where you two come in."

"What do you mean? And why do you care anyway? The school has nothing to do with you!" Erin interjected.

Cara suddenly stood and walked over to her rucksack. She pulled it open, rifled through until she found a wallet. Opening it, she stared down and then in contrast to her icy manner, tears melted down her face as though she was thawing out. The Ice Queen did seem to have emotions, Erin thought. Cara stroked the inside of the wallet gently. "Little Georgie," she whispered, almost to herself.

They were all silent. Mal and Erin looked at each other, Mal shrugged his shoulders and Erin raised her eyebrows back at him. Mal stood and put his arm around the weeping girl, and she turned and fell into his arms sobbing. As she did so she dropped the wallet onto the ground below. Erin reached over and scooped it up. A young boy grinned back at her with dimples in his round pink cheeks. He held a wooden train in one hand, and he was sitting on a fat tree trunk. The bright sunshine behind him lit up his blonde hair. He looked about four years old.

Cara finally stopped crying and sat down again. She blew her nose, and wiped tears of pain away. "He's my little brother," she explained. "Was my little brother. He died shortly after that was taken. Meningitis. One moment he was there and the next he was gone."

"I'm so sorry, Cara. I had no idea." Erin felt guilty for not trusting her. She handed back the picture.

"Me too. That must have been awful for you and your parents." Mal knelt and took her tiny white hands into his large tanned ones.

"My mother couldn't cope. Dad was very patient with her, he was grieving too, but seemed to cope with it because of his work." Cara was silent, her eyes looked away in the distance, a distant past that the others knew nothing about. Mal stroked her hand gently and this seemed to make her return to the present. "She died six months after Georgie. A car crash, head on collision. She was on the wrong side of the road. Dad said Mum had been drinking that night and there was nothing anyone could do."

Cara wiped her tears away and blew her nose. "At least they are together now; Mum and George. Dad and I have each other."

Erin stood and grabbed the kettle and stumbled

out of the tent, her own tears coming thick and fast now. She needed to be alone with her own thoughts. There was a heavy ache in the very depths of her stomach. So much to take in. A picture of home and Mum and Dad came to her as she stood over the water tap in the tiny corrugated shed, filling the kettle and wishing she was at home in their kitchen watching Dad baking chocolate muffins – their favourite. Freezing water pouring down onto her shoes shocked her into the present and she grabbed the stiff brass tap trying desperately to turn off the waterfall. It wouldn't budge; the concrete floor was soon flooded. Erin grabbed the overflowing kettle and squelched back to the tent, shouting to Mal to come and help.

Later, that night, once everyone was tucked up in their sleeping bags, Erin scanned her text messages, but there was nothing from Petra. She was relieved but felt sad too. Her friend would have been good at cheering her up, with her silly jokes about the teachers at school – she was brilliant at doing impressions and took off Mr Gunn, their maths teacher, particularly well, especially when he was having a stammering fit. It was unfortunate he had problems with the letter S, when he had to teach statistics and sums and signs and symbols.

Erin smiled at her memories, but that hollow feeling soon returned, and she sighed. Anyway, she thought some people have a lot worse to put up with in life. Cara, for example, was living with the pain every day of losing not only her brother but her mother too. Why did she show us the photo and tell us that story? Erin thought.

Suddenly she sat bolt upright. What has all that got to do with the school? Cara never explained the link. She never answers questions; she seems to skirt round things until you have forgotten what you asked in the first place. Erin's mind was full of thoughts and images that seemed to merge and change like a child's kaleidoscope. The more she tried to work things out the more confused she became. Right, she said to herself, let's think logically about what I do know. She began to make bullet points onto her phone.

- I have a twin sister – Miranda.
- She looks like me.
- Mum and Dad see her every 5 years.
- Mum has pictures of Miranda taken in exotic places. (This one she'd worked out after concluding she wasn't going mad and forgotten visiting these places).
- We watched black cars leave the hotel and disappear at the farm. (We never actually saw Miranda in one of the cars).
- We know there is a school in an old, disused underground bunker. (Or do we? Erin wasn't sure whether to believe Cara on this).

Erin began a new list – Questions

- Is Miranda in the hotel/country house we visited?
- Is M in the farmhouse?
- Is M in an underground school?
- What is the connection between Cara and Miranda? (And little George).
- What is our next step? (Go and watch the farm and visit the hotel place again).

Erin snuggled down into her sleeping bag; she was beginning to feel sleepy. Tomorrow, I will have all the answers. I will find my sister and we will be friends. With those thoughts Erin closed her eyes and slept.

Chapter 10

 Z89 had been woken by the sound of the uniform drawer clicking open. Struggling to open her eyes, she climbed out of her bunk and pulled out the clothing. GREY. Her heart sank. I have been working so hard recently, keeping my head down, even Miss Citrine and Mr Garnet commented on how much I was improving in their lessons. Z89 slumped down on the tiny area of floor of the pod; tears came quickly and silently. I will never be good enough, no one cares about me, about any of us here. The morning chant of "we are loved" sounded over and over in her head. What is love? she thought. What does it mean to belong?

Later, as she sat with her cohort of ten students in the Nourishment Sector, she looked at the five boys and four girls. They were all Marcon, but that was the only link - all born on the same day - March 1st, 2000 - all educated the same, all shown the same care and attention and yet there was something more that Z89 felt singled each one out.

Each one of them had an identity that couldn't be taken away from them, something innate, something that showed they were special.

"Z89 Marcon, go to the door of the Central Hub." The voice came over the speakers. The others all looked at her, shocked. It was very rare that anyone went there. That was the place of legends, people told you it was heaven compared to this hell, an oasis in a desert, but there were scorpions there that could poison your mind and body - even worse than the Correction Sector.

Walking along the corridor, she felt nervous. Her palms were damp with sweat, her heart quickening. Why was she being summoned? Z89 stopped in front of a huge white door which slid open with a gentle swooshing sound and she stepped into an area that reminded her of a cathedral, having visited one in the Enrichment Sector. The walls around her, were constructed from white marble and rose high to the sky above; natural light shining down. A tinkling sound to her right made her look across to a waterfall that cascaded down a glass wall into a trough full of lush green plants.

A scrawny, gunmetal-grey haired woman, an Administrator, dressed in a beige suit, gestured for her to follow her. They stopped outside an oak door, a symmetrical pattern of squares and circles carved into the wood. The woman knocked and a syrupy voice came dripping through the door,

"You may enter," and the door was opened.

"Ah, Z89. A pleasure to see you my child." The sweet smell of roses and lilies invaded her senses as Z89 entered, the brightness making her blink repeatedly. She stretched her eyes wider and then allowed them to look in the direction of the beautiful aroma. A huge floral arrangement stood majestically on a side table. Towering shelves engorged with books of every size and colour, filled the walls. Pens and pencils sat upright in colourful pots and piles of neatly stacked paper lay on another side table. The main desk was a solid oak table with a laptop, phone and a wooden box and nothing else. As Z89 stood there she was suddenly aware of a statuesque golden time piece that was enclosed in a tower of dark wood; the clock face seemed to peer down at her from its lofty height.

"Good morning, Miss Dorling." Z89 was polite and outwardly calm, but inside butterflies fluttered against her heart, boats tossed on the stormy sea of her stomach.

"I detest mess and bad organisation, don't you?" The woman in purple, sitting behind the desk, stared at the girl in front of her.,

"Yes, Miss Dorling."

Suddenly, the purple figure stood and swept across to the huge vase of flowers. She lifted a fallen petal, tutted and threw it into a wooden bin at the side of her desk.

She turned, like a cobra, seeking its prey. "I also hate insubordination. This, for example." She lifted the lid of the box that sat squarely on her desk. She held out a tiny paper boat. Z89 gasped. How did she find that?

"We have been doing Pod inspections."

"But, but that's my private space."

"Nothing here is private, child." The syrup oozed once again from her tongue.

Without warning, the cobra struck – she put both hands into the box and lifted out a whole ocean of paper boats, all covered in tiny writing, and threw them at the girl before her. They fell around her like dead butterflies. One seemed to perch on her shoulder before upending and sinking to the ground.

"What is the meaning of this?" Miss Dorling spat the words into the young girl's face, spittle ran down a pale cheek and mingled with tears. "Expect a very severe punishment this time, Z89 Marcon." The woman sneered as she returned to her chair.

Z89 stood, her head bowed. In one hand she held one small boat she'd caught and saved from the storm created by the woman before her. Silently, she folded her fingers over it and held it tight.

Miss Dorling bent over papers on her desk and didn't look up as she said, "You will give us feedback about this experience to help with our research." Then, she raised her head, stared straight into the girl's eyes and added maliciously, "That is of course, if you survive."

 They set off early the next morning, a pink haze framed the distant horizon. They couldn't agree between themselves of where to start first. Erin suggested they visit the place where she had first seen Miranda. "Perhaps the school is part of the building. We can't say for sure that Miranda was in one of those black cars."

Mal and Cara looked at her. Mal said, "I'd never thought of that. What do you think, Cara?"

Erin was irritated that Mal seemed to always be asking Cara for her opinion. Now the young woman said, "I don't know. Dad and I are pretty sure there's something suspicious about the farm. I think that is where we should go this morning."

Mal agreed and the decision had been made, much to Erin's annoyance. So here they were driving along narrow lanes with high banked up sides, Erin slumped in the back nibbling a biscuit and Mal and Cara chatting to each other as if they had known each other for ever. Erin felt she was the outsider, she didn't belong, as though her ideas didn't matter. A sharp question from Cara broke into her thoughts.

"What are you doing, Mal?"

Mal turned down a road that came long before the lane to the farm. "I had a look on Google maps last night and thought we ought to check out the area around the farm."

Cara seemed unsettled; someone had gone against what she'd said. "Oh!" was all she could say. Then she smiled, "Alright, whatever you think is best, love." Cara stroked Mal's arm and he grinned back.

In the back seat, Erin squirmed at the sickly-sweet voice.

The early morning mists strewn across the land like cobwebs were now beginning to clear and the sky gradually turned from coal black to slate grey. In the growing light they could make out huge banks of chocolate brown earth rising from the ground, barbed wire fences that ran parallel to the road and small, metal signs at various intervals informing them that the spiky barrier was electrified. Further along they came to a huge sign,

DANGER. NO ENTRY
This land belongs to MOD
KEEP OUT

Erin wasn't sure what MOD meant, but Mal explained it stood for Ministry of Defence. He knew the army used some of the moor to practise their manoeuvres. They continued along the twisty road, coming across more signs that repeated the warning, until they had done several miles encircling the farm and eventually returning to the main road. By the time they stopped near the turning to the farm, the sky had been painted in a watery blue by an unseen hand.

Erin's phone beeped, a text message.

Just checking on you. Hope M is looking after you. Love Mum xxx

Erin quickly replied, trying not to feel guilty about lying to her parents and then noticed the date on her screen, April 1st. A month since my birthday. They had been here a month ago and perhaps now they would find Miranda.

Mal climbed out of the car, but as he did so, a shiny black car appeared at the end of the lane. He hurriedly clambered back in and urged the girls to duck down. From the back seat, Erin peeped out and watched as the car glided past them followed by two further cars; all identical, just like the ones they had seen a month ago.

"Mal, we must follow them. Miranda might be in one of those cars." She grasped her brother's shoulder and shook him hard.

He turned the car and they began to follow at a distance. After a few miles, the entourage turned into a tree lined road, the branches now smothered with pink blossom. It was the same place they had seen Miranda meet their parents.

Mal pulled into a shady spot and they quickly climbed out. Keeping close together, they ran in convoy under the cover of the trees and bushes. A riot of pink, purple and white frothy flowers, surrounded them like huge marshmallows. They stopped at the edge of the wood and watched in amazement, as three adults, one dressed in green, one in yellow and another in orange alighted from the front passenger door of each of the cars. From the rear doors came ten young people, five boys, five girls. All dressed in colourful outfits that looked a bit dated to Erin. She strained to see if Miranda was with them, but she wasn't there.

The adults led the young people through the open doors. Two men stood either side of the entrance, their stance aggressive and sinister. Their dark glasses caught the sun and it danced on the handle of revolvers protruding from their belts. The cars rolled on round out of sight behind the building.

"When I saw Miranda, there were ten kids with their parents." Erin started to describe what she had seen previously, but Cara hushed her, much to Erin's annoyance. Mal grabbed her shoulder and pulled her down. "What the ..." she threw back at them.

"Look!" Cara pointed towards another car pulling into the car park, and then another and another. Out of each stepped two adults – a man and a woman – and after walking off they could be seen to be welcomed into the building. Erin quickly counted the cars. Ten cars.

They waited but no one else arrived. There was a silence that evaded their space and their thoughts, like enemy soldiers infiltrating the trenches of their mind. Without speaking, the three of them stumbled back to the car.

"What does it all mean?" Mal asked, speaking to no one in particular.

Cara spoke. "I have watched this happen before. It was the 1st of February. I remember the date clearly, because it would have been Georgie's birthday.

"Today is 1st April," Erin added. "And my birthday is 1st March. This can't be coincidence. We must find out what this all has to do with Miranda and what is happening here in Cornwall." What they had witnessed, made her more determined than ever to find out the truth.

It was getting close to noon when they arrived back at the farm. They could hear a tractor ploughing up and down a distant field, blackbirds were singing in the trees and sheep were bleating beyond a high hedge. A calm, rural scene. Nothing strange. Erin scrambled out of the little car and stretched her legs. She ran across to a high bank of ground, struggled to the top ridge and then turned towards the horizon. Far beyond in the distance a blue ribbon of sea could be seen between the headland and the cliffs. It beckoned her, and memories of family holidays there in the little bay flooded her head. They had only been a few miles from Miranda, and she had never known of her existence. Perhaps that was why her mum and dad kept on returning to this area. From this vantage point, Erin realised, turning, that she could see into the farmyard quite clearly. She shaded her eyes as she saw yet another black car parked outside the house.

Hurriedly, she ran back to the others. "There's another car!" she said breathlessly.

Cara and Mal were sitting close together, their heads touching, Cara whispering into Mal's ear. Erin shoved her brother and he started. "Get off Erin. Stop being such a pain!" He was obviously annoyed with her for invading their privacy.

"Mal, please," she entreated him. "I need you to help me." Erin looked so distraught Mal stood and went to her.

He sighed. "What have you seen?"

"A car, outside the house. But this is different. I think it's a hearse. I think someone is dead."

Clouds seemed to lift from his eyes, and he ran to the top of the bank. Erin trailed after him.

"I think you're right, sis."

"What if it's Miranda?" She grabbed his arm tightly and looked into his eyes.

"I'm sure she is fine." He began to say something more, but Erin squeezed his arm and pointed. They stood and watched as two funeral directors, each wearing tailcoats and top hats, came out of the house and climbed into the hearse. They made their way down the road and out onto the lane passing Cara and the little Fiat.

"I know that funeral directors', they're based in Castleton," Cara said as they came back down towards her. "I recognise the woman. She was there when George and Mum passed away. She was lovely and kind towards me."

"It's a way in," Erin announced.

"What?" Mal replied. "We can't go in pretending to be funeral directors." He laughed, and Cara joined in.

"No, one of us can go in the empty coffin. Then we can be taken in and wait until it's quiet and …"

"Jump out and go, surprise! Oh, for God's sake Erin, this isn't a time for a circus trick." Cara poured scorn on to Erin's enthusiasm.

"Hold on, Cara, I think she's got something. Also, if you know that lady, she might be able to help us. We'll have to decide who can go in. I don't really fancy being put inside a coffin and having it nailed down."

"It has to be me," Erin said determined to be the one in the wooden box. "I want to find Miranda more than anyone."

"So, what are you going to do when you get in there?" scoffed Cara. "You're going to need some help in that place." She looked at Erin with hooded eyes. "You're planning to get her out, aren't you?

You must be mad!"

"I just want to speak to her. I want her to know I'm her twin. If she's not happy here, then we can try and get her out. She can come and live with us and go to school with me."

"I think, darlin' you are living in cloud cuckoo land." Cara climbed back in the car and went to slam the door to end the conversation, however Erin stood in her way.

"What about George? What has he got to do with all this?" Erin thrust her face into Cara's. "Is he in there too? Does he have a twin?" She grabbed the older girl's collar and using her karate strength and skills, pulled her out of the car. She pushed Cara against the Fiat and held her arms down forcibly. "You said you would help us."

Cara kicked wildly and pulled away from the smaller girl's grasp, but Erin was too quick for her. She blocked the kicks with her arms and then punched Cara squarely in the stomach who immediately doubled up and fell to her knees, coughing, winded.

"That's enough, you two." Mal went to Cara and held her. "Fighting isn't going to help Miranda, is it?"

Erin stepped away from them, panting heavily. Tears were pricking at her eyes and she brushed them angrily away. Suddenly, she felt all the fight flow out of her, and she slumped against the car.

"We need to think this through properly and plan. Otherwise we could put you and Miranda in danger," Mal said urging them into the car and then driving in silence back to the campsite.

After arriving back Mal and Cara prepared some food – hot dogs – while Erin threw herself onto her sleeping bag and began scrolling through her phone. She finally emerged when Mal stuck his head into her sleeping area and told her to grow up, to get out here now and to eat. Erin decided to pretend everything was okay, and mumbled an apology, but inside she didn't like how Cara was treating her.

They decided they didn't have many options open to them. Erin wanted to go and knock on the door of the farm or the hotel and try and talk their way in, but Mal reminded her of the guards with guns. Then, she suggested again her idea of hiding in a coffin, but the others weren't so sure. "Anyway, there can't be that many deaths in a school, surely," Mal added when they were discussing it. "Won't they think it odd that another coffin is suddenly delivered?"

Over a mug of coffee, Cara finally told them about her little brother. Mal and Erin sat and listened. She explained that when her mother died, her father discovered various documents, one of which was a contract pertaining to the sale of one male baby and a copy of a birth certificate for Frankie Mallory born 1st February 2000, at two minutes past four. He didn't tell Cara about this at the time, they were both grieving in their own way, but when she was fourteen, he sat her down and told her everything.

According to Cara, her father had known there was a twin, he watched them both being born, but in the hospital the baby became very ill and the nurses had taken the baby off to a special incubator. Her father described carrying the tiny coffin into a church full of people crying. He and Cara's mother agreed to not tell their daughter about the baby as they didn't want to upset her; they brought up George as their only son.

Her father told her that just after George was born, an aunt of her mother's left her a considerable amount of money. This is what she had told him. The amount written in the contract of the sale of a baby boy was the same amount of the aunt's legacy.

Erin couldn't believe what she was telling them. Cara's mother sold her baby just like her own parents had done. What is wrong with these people? She thought to herself.

Cara went on to explain that her father spent the last few years trying to find out where Frankie had been taken. He believed so strongly Frankie was in this underground school that he and Cara moved to Castleton to be closer.

"Your dad would have been invited to the birthday meal, like our parents were," suggested Erin. "They have been coming here every five years to see Miranda."

"No, he has never seen his son and I have not seen my brother," Cara replied wistfully.

Erin suddenly felt overwhelmed with guilt. She rushed over to Cara and hugged her. "I'm so sorry ... for everything." Cara was stiff in the embrace but then seemed to relax. Erin carried on, "But, this makes me even more determined to find Miranda and now Frankie." Another memory sidled up to her. "Oh no! Petra! She has a sister there too."

"We're not going to be able to get them all out, Erin." Mal was adamant. "I don't think we can even get in there."

"But we have to try. Please, we must try something." Erin pleaded with her brother.

"Alright," said Cara. "I have another idea." They listened carefully and then began to plan their next move. It was far into the night by the time they were satisfied they had something that could work. It could be dangerous, but Erin was determined to find Miranda.

Chapter 11

 Z89, professing her innocence, had been dragged from Miss Dorling's room. She knew deep in her heart what she'd done was against the rules but couldn't see why it mattered so much. No one was allowed books, paper or writing materials in their Pod; this was strictly forbidden. Books, students studied in lessons, had been vetted for their content and only certain texts were available to them, and then for a limited time before being locked away. No one was to write such emotional words as she had done, covering every millimetre of paper before folding them up.

When asked about the boat shape, Z89 was slow to respond, but then explained the kind man always made her a paper boat and wrote messages inside. She'd seen boats on the ocean in documentaries they had been allowed to watch. They always looked free bobbing about on the water, she wanted to feel free like that.

The room she was thrown into was empty apart

from a high desk with a computer sitting on the top. The desk was set inside a glass compartment. The main door clicked open and an Orderly in a brown uniform entered. He stepped inside the glass box and closed the door. Standing at the controls the man looked blankly at Z89 before putting on ear defenders. Then without warning he flicked a switch and freezing, icy water entered the room in torrents from either side of where Z89 stood. Tumbling over when the hard jets hit her, she struggled to stand.

Boiling hot water then followed. The drenched girl was scalded, her skin turning scarlet. The water was turned off and red-hot lamps opened in the ceiling, bearing down heavily onto her already sore body. "No, please, stop!" she screamed trying to protect herself with her arms, but to no avail and blisters began to form on her pale skin. The lamps snapped off and an icy wind blew from fans. Now, she was shaking, her teeth chattering.

The sequence was repeated, again and again and again until finally the lights went out apart from one tiny red light on the Orderly's computer. Z89's heart pounded hard against her ribs, her breath coming in short gasps and then when she thought it was all over, belting loud music belched out of loudspeakers. The floor seemed to reverberate and Z89 held her hands against her ears. An excruciating pain twisted inside her ear drums and she dropped to the floor with a scream.

Bright light returned as the noise was shut off; the girl shaded her eyes from the white rays that threatened to blind her. Exhausted, Z89 lay on the tiled floor panting. She couldn't speak.

"Leave the room now, Z89!" instructed the robotic Orderly. A door to her right clicked open and she crawled towards it, every movement agony, every touch a torment. She entered a small cell, with a bed, a sink and toilet and nothing else. The door closed behind her. Collapsing on to the bed, hardly breathing, her skin red raw, her throat dry Z89 lay as still as a corpse in a mortuary.

Erin sat waiting in the front seat of the car for Cara and Mal to return. They were in the funeral directors' offices in Castleton, talking to the woman that Cara knew. Last night, they argued over different scenarios, but they kept coming back to the coffin. This woman could access the building and could help them if she could be persuaded to do so.

Playing a game on her phone, eyes glued firmly to the screen, Erin pulled open the glove compartment and searched blindly with one hand for some sweets. Her hand rifled over scrunched up paper bags, a throwaway cup and a book of some sort until she touched a small box. Grabbing it, she missed wildly with her shot as she pulled out a tiny silver box. The gift Mum and Dad gave to Miranda on her birthday. She'd totally forgotten about it. She abandoned the game and carefully opened the lid. Inside, nestled in pale pink tissue paper was an exquisite silver and white enamel brooch in the shape of a butterfly. It was a replica of the one her parents had given her for her birthday. She held her breath and gently stroked the wings. Butterflies meant freedom. Erin was still staring at the brooch when someone slammed their hand hard against the window. She jumped and dropped the box. The butterfly flew out, tissue paper fell and a tiny paper boat sailed to the floor.

"Only me," said Mal pulling back the driver's seat to allow Cara to struggle into the back of the car before sliding down into his seat.

Erin hit her brother hard on the arm. "You scared me, you idiot." She scooped up all the debris from the box. The paper boat had tiny writing on it.

"What have you got there?" Mal asked.

"This was the gift Miranda was given. There's a note inside."

"Well come on then. What does it say?"

I saw you. Help me. Z89 Marcon.

"What does it mean?" enquired Mal, taking the boat into his hands and reading it to himself. "Hey, Dad makes these."

"I know he does, but the message must be from Miranda. She must have seen me at the hotel that day."

"What does the last bit, Z89, mean? Is that a code for something? Perhaps it's a code for getting in. Marcon? Is that a name?" Mal fired questions back at his sister.

"I think she's in danger," Erin added. "She's asking for help."

Mal sighed, "True."

A voice from the back seat reminded Erin that Cara was still with them. "Can we eat now? I'm starving." Erin rolled her eyes and bit her lip, annoyed with the interruption, but her stomach growled in agreement with the others. She had to admit; she could do with some food.

"Good idea, Cara," Mal answered starting the car. "Then we can tell Erin what we found out."

They drove to a small café further down into the town and after ordering burgers, chips and mugs of steaming hot tea, Cara gave an account of what they had discovered at the funeral directors.

"It's not going to work. Even though she remembered me, Pandora – that's her name – said that it wasn't ethical, and she would lose her job."

They had reached another dead end. They finished their food in silence, all thinking of ideas of what to do next.

"You were right, Cara. It was a stupid idea." Erin hated to admit she was wrong. She began to wonder if she was ever going to see her sister. Perhaps, Mum and Dad were right, we would have to wait until we were 18 and then she would be free. Until then, we would both be prisoners of our lives. A jangle of sounds interrupted her thoughts and she grabbed her phone, not really noticing the caller ID, she touched the green circle.

"Hi Erin, it's me. Please don't hang up. I need you." Petra's breathless voice came to her through the ether of the phone world.

Erin replied after a few seconds. "Hi Petra. Okay."

"There's something you must know about Shay and me."

Erin took a deep breath. "It's okay. I know. I saw you together. I heard every word. Don't worry about me, I hope you'll be very happy together."

"Oh, I see. Well in that case, you'll understand." Petra went quiet and then. "Where are you? Your mum said you were in Wales, but I've checked your location on my phone."

"We're in Cornwall. But you mustn't tell my mum and dad. They can't find out." Erin felt a strange detachment from her friend. Someone she thought she could trust and who had betrayed her. She looked across at Cara, who was leaning into Mal. He was telling her a joke and they giggled like little children. Cara, who she thought she shouldn't trust turned out to be on her side; her guardian angel.

"Are you trying to see your sister, Erin? Does she exist?"

"That's what we would like to do, but …" she tailed off.

"But, what, Erin?" Petra asked. "Are you okay? I miss you. I miss your friendship."

"I miss you too. Petra, there's something I need to tell you." Erin paused, her breath coming slow and shallow as she thought about what she was going to say. "You have a twin too. She's here in Cornwall." Then, it all came pouring out like water rushing through a crack in a dam. Once the dam had been breached, there was no going back.

"Petra, are you still there? Speak to me ... please." Erin was scared now. Mal reached across and stroked her arm. He and Cara had been listening to the one-sided conversation and now they waited for Erin to hang up.

The silence from the other end of the line stretched into what seemed like an eternity. Then a small sob, followed by loud sniffing sounds, emitted from the phone. "I'm so sorry, Petra. I had to keep it a secret. Just like you and Shay kept your secret from me."

The sobs subsided and then Petra spoke in a distant, dreamlike voice. "Thank you for telling me. Goodbye Erin." The phone went dead.

"Petra? Speak to me." Erin jabbed at the touchscreen with her finger but Petra's number was engaged.

"What a mess!" She threw her phone onto the table where it bounced and then fell to the floor. Mal retrieved it, the screen was smashed and black. "Brilliant, that's all I need!" she shouted, suddenly standing, knocking over her unfinished tea. "I can't cope with all this anymore." She stomped out of the café, out on to the street and started walking blindly towards who knew where.

Erin passed some shops and a pub and soon found herself outside a church. Before she knew what she was doing she was stumbling through the churchyard to a wrought iron bench, surrounded by daffodils; their yellow and orange heads bobbing in the breeze. There, she sank down and the floodgates opened. The tears poured from her eyes, the ache in her stomach grew, she felt hot and cold at the same time and her skin burned. "I'm so useless. I can't do anything right."

"Can I help you, dear?" A gentle voice came from behind. "I'm sure you're not useless at all." Erin hadn't realised she'd spoken out loud.

"There, there, my dear. Let it all out." A shadow fell across the bench and an arm wound around Erin. It belonged to an elderly lady wearing a mustard yellow felt hat, a bright turquoise coat and matching scarf. Erin sobbed into her shoulder, and the lady passed her an embroidered handkerchief that smelt faintly of lavender. Calmness washed over her and she sat back, wiping her eyes and blowing her nose.

"Thank you," she sniffed.

"I know what it's like when grief hits you. It's like a whirlwind that punches you in the stomach. You have to ride the storm and then the sun will come out again." At that, the sun suddenly pushed its way out from behind the steel grey clouds. "There you see, what did I tell you? There's always sunshine after the rain. I'm Elsie, by the way."

Erin introduced herself between sniffs. She tried to hand back the wet hankie, but Elsie insisted she kept it. "Why is everything so difficult?" Erin asked.

Elsie smiled, her face crinkling as she did so. Her brown eyes sparkled under the rim of her hat. "So that we can learn, my dear. Life would be very boring if everything was easy. We have all had to learn to walk and run, to speak and shout, to accept and understand." Elsie patted her hand, the mottled, wrinkled hand against the smooth skin of youth. "You're a fighter, my girl."

Erin smiled at that. Yes, she was a fighter and in the true sense of the word. Learning Japanese and how to defend herself against her opponents had taught her many things: humility, determination and strength of character. Erin pulled herself up, dropped her shoulders and breathed in deeply. "Thank you, Elsie."

They both sat in silence for a while enjoying the warmth of the Spring sunshine. That was where Malachi and Cara found her, sitting next to a grey-haired lady. Introductions were made, hugs were given and received, and words of thanks passed between them.

"Cara Mallory?" mused Elsie. "Are you Professor Mallory's daughter?"

"Yes, I am." Cara looked confused for a moment, narrowing her eyes and then asked sharply, "How do you know my father?"

Elsie, peering at Cara, explained. "I used to work at the laboratory, a long time ago. He was a brilliant scientist. How is he?"

Cara said her father was well and then looked

across at Mal and nodded. He seemed to take the hint. "Well, lovely to meet you, Elsie. We must get going. Thank you for looking after Erin." He and Cara turned towards the main gate and began to walk away hand in hand.

Before joining them, Erin hugged the old lady and thanked her again. Elsie whispered into her ear, "Watch that one my dear. If she is anything like her father, I wouldn't trust her. Don't turn your back on her, believe me." Elsie gripped Erin's arm tightly. "Remember this."

Erin nodded and turned away. She fell in step with the others as they left the churchyard and Cara put her arm around her. "We were so worried about you. You're safe now, my lovely girl."

They turned into the camp-site entrance, drove slowly over the bumpy ground towards their bright blue and green tent, to find a strange man waiting for them. The sky was now overcast, leaden with the portent of rain; the wind had grown from a whisper to a shout. Branches were being whipped by gusts, and the tent complaining of the force, pulled at its ropes.

The man wore a long brown tweed coat and was bare headed. His eyes were sad, and his face drooped, but he stood stiffly upright.

"Pandora sent me. She says yes. Be at the funeral parlour tomorrow morning at eight, sharp."

"What made her change her mind?" Cara asked, placing her hand on his arm.

The man flinched as though he'd been burnt. "She didn't say." He turned smartly and walked away, his body bending against the wind. The three of them stared after him as he squeezed himself into the tiny front seat of a silver mini, incongruous to the man, and drove away.

That night the storm raged, railing against the canvas. The rain and wind slammed hard, buffeting the defenceless tent, while they lay huddled in their sleeping bags. Forked lightning filled the sky cracking the clouds apart to allow hail to pelt them. Erin hoped this wasn't a bad omen for the next day but couldn't stop a horrible feeling of foreboding creep up and over her body. She slept fitfully and dreamless, waking to the calm of the morning and first light stretching across the hedges and trees.

They arrived just before eight and knocked on the door. It creaked open, and Pandora stepped back to let them in. Placing a stubby finger against her lips she beckoned them to follow her. She stopped in front of a pale blue door and unlocked it before ushering them all in. It was only when they were all in the darkened room that she spoke.

"I thought over what you said," she began. "I knew Cara's mother, Jess, very well and was devastated when she died. I decided that I should help." As she said this, she flicked a switch, spotlights set into the ceiling shone down and now they could see the wooden coffin perched on a low table covered with a gold cloth. The lid was off, and they could make out the golden silk lining that swathed the inside. An opening in the wall beyond, allowed coffins to be transferred directly into the back of a hearse.

"Do you think this will work?" asked Erin going to the coffin and feeling the inside.

"Who knows? But it's worth a try." Pandora answered briskly. She showed Erin the tiny holes in the lid that had been drilled to allow her to breathe. "I have been inside the school," she announced. Erin and the others looked at her in surprise.

"Please tell us what you have seen?" Mal asked urgently. He wanted to make sure Erin would be safe. He couldn't face having to explain to his parents they had lost her too.

"Not much I'm afraid. There is a lift that goes from inside the farmhouse that takes you down into the Central Hub. It's beautiful there." She described the many lush plants and a waterfall that tumbled down a glass wall. "The only other space I saw was the medical room and mortuary. White and spotless. I will be able to take you in there, Erin and help you out of the coffin. You are on your own then I'm afraid."

Now, the moment finally arrived and Erin found herself anxious. "You don't have to do this," Mal urged. "Are you sure she'll be okay in there?"

he asked Pandora. Erin stared at the thin woman dressed in a black tailcoat and long skirt. Her eyes were full of sadness.

"I don't know. What I do know is how it feels when you lose someone you love." Pandora didn't elaborate on her statement apart from saying, "I want to help, that is all."

"We have no other choice," Erin announced. "We have to give this a try."

Mal sighed and pulled his sister towards him. She hugged him tightly and then glancing over to Cara who stood there with a strange look on her face, a slight smile at one corner of her mouth and her eyes narrowing, Erin climbed up into the coffin. She shuddered as she lay down and Pandora passed her a bottle of water and small torch. Mal passed her his phone. "You're going to need this. Cara's number is on there. Keep in contact."

Erin grimaced as the lid came down and screws crunched and groaned into the panels of the coffin. She held her breath in a panic and wanted to scream but counted slowly to 10 and her breathing calmed. Erin had to trust Pandora now. Being blind to what was happening, her hearing seemed to become more acute as she tried to work out the sounds around her. Erin felt the coffin slide, feet first and stop, a car engine revved loudly and they were off.

After a restless night, Erin was exhausted and the gentle humming and rolling of the car rocked her to sleep. In a dream-like state she felt herself being pulled backwards, and then skinny shafts of sunlight that lanced through the air holes, pricked her face. She was out of the hearse. A rasp of metal, a squeaking of a wheel and a sudden wobble made her realise the coffin had been placed on a trolley.

Rubbing her eyes, she was aware of voices and the sound of a lift opening and closing. Her stomach twisted as the coffin lurched forward and then she was aware of going down, a rattling and rocking increasing her fear they had arrived and were going underground. Sounds became muffled until she made herself yawn and her ears popped.

Footsteps clicked on hard floors and soft voices wafted alongside her but the words were indistinct to Erin hidden away like a corpse. What if they leave me in here? I'm so hot. I can't breathe. Her heart banged against her ribs, her chest tightening like a vice. I mustn't panic.

Closing her eyes, she told herself to move through a karate kata in her mind; something she often did at the dentist to stay calm. Doors opened and slammed shut, more voices and then finally the turning of the screws, and the lid was removed from the box. The relief on seeing Pandora looking down on her, brought tears. Erin wiped them away roughly.

"Hope will always be with you, even when you meet demons," Pandora said helping Erin up, who stood blinking taking in her surroundings. She started as she turned and saw the man who had come to the camp site. "Edward, you have met already," Pandora said. Edward, dressed in a brown uniform from head to foot held out a white uniform and shoes for Erin.

"He works here," she explained.

"Are we safe? Was anyone suspicious?"

"Yes, we're safe. It all went smoothly. Edward met us at the car and helped me bring you in. Now, get dressed, we don't have much time." Edward turned away so that Erin could change.

"Who is dead?" Erin asked quietly.

"A young woman, I believe. Z89." Edward replied.

Erin recognised the number – she pulled out the paper boat and read the message. She let out a small sob. "Is it Miranda?" she asked holding her breath. She thought, if I can hold my breath until the answer comes it won't be her.

The silence seemed interminable as Edward checked through his paperwork. "No. Miranda is Marcon, this one is Z89 Septcon," he announced.

Erin breathed out and relaxed for a moment or two. Thank goodness, she thought, but immediately felt bad another girl had died. "Do you know how she died?" she asked.

"No time for that now. You must hurry as they will be bringing in the body soon," Pandora said earnestly, gesturing towards Erin to dress faster.

Edward passed her a nylon cap. "Put this on.

You will blend in if you look like you have no hair."
Erin was shocked. "What do you mean?"

"All our students' heads are shaved. It removes their identity and makes them more servile."

"That's horrible. That's what the Nazis did in concentration camps! Why on earth …"

Pandora interrupted her. "Please, Erin – you must put it on." She took the cap and slid it over Erin's head, then she carefully tucked in her long hair. "Now, you must go." Erin winced, patting her head encased in nylon. Pandora awkwardly pulled Erin towards her saying, "Go and find your sister. You can do this."

A door slid open in the wall and Edward indicated for her to leave. "You will find Z89 in the Correction Sector, in solitary confinement," he murmured. "Follow the signs."

Wandering along a brightly lit corridor, Erin found herself beginning to panic. This time she used her karate skill of Zanshin, a heightened awareness of her surroundings. She concentrated on her breathing and made herself relax while remaining alert. Keeping close to the wall, Erin tried to look confident. A line of boys and girls, all dressed in white just like her, was coming towards her. No one spoke. She didn't know whether she should say anything. In the end as they passed her, she fell into step behind the last person. They continued walking and then turned into a room with a sign that said, THE LEARNING LAB. Erin left the group and carried on past glancing into the room. Inside were several compartments fitted against a wall – in each one a student now sat facing a desk and a computer screen. Just like my school, she thought.

Erin continued to walk along the corridor. There was no artwork on the walls, no colour anywhere and she realised there were only a few adults around. Occasionally she saw in the distance other students, some in grey or blue being led by people in brown uniforms. The ones in grey looked sad, some even appeared scared. Erin wondered where they were going and decided to follow the grey line of four students with a man dressed in brown, just like Edward.

They entered an area that had wooden cell doors with small round windows cut into them. The sign said CORRECTION SECTOR and Erin's heart began to race. This was what she'd been looking for. Edward had said Miranda was here.

Each student was taken into a cell and the door locked behind them. Erin hid behind a stone pillar until the man in brown had gone. She waited a few moments and then tiptoed across to the cell doors and peered inside. One young person was in each, sitting forlornly on a hard bed. No one looked up at the elfin face that appeared at the glass, until she came to a cell away from the others. Here in the farthest corner of the space, Erin stared through the window and her own face stared back at her.

Erin blinked in surprise and the girl on the other side of the door blinked in unison. The girl, an exact copy of Erin apart from her hair, stood and hobbled, as though in pain, to the door. She held out her fingers and laid them on the glass. Erin placed her own fingers like a reflection.

"Miranda," she whispered. "I am your sister, Erin."

Chapter 12

 Z89 stared when her reflected self, touched the glass from the other side of the door. The cold hard barrier was the only thing between them.

"I am Z89," she whispered. "How did you get here?"

She found she could just about make out what the other girl was saying. She seemed to be saying her name was Erin and that she was her sister. Well, of course she is, thought Z89. I knew that straightaway as soon as I saw her in the restaurant when I was with those two nice people with the sad eyes.

Erin was speaking again. "I've come to find you and get you out of here, if I can."

Z89 smiled at this, but with no real conviction. She knew there was no escape. "It's not safe here. You are in danger. They must not find you here."

The other girl held up a tiny paper boat. "I want to help you sail away from here." Erin made the boat look as if it was bobbing up and down on the sea. Z89 laughed, something she very rarely did, and Erin joined in. There was a bond between them and Z89 knew instinctively it could never be broken now they had found each other.

Z89 suddenly bent over and coughed, her body aching from the punishment she endured the day before. Her skin was slowly beginning to heal, after an Orderly had checked on her, applying ointment to her burns. Painkillers were handed over too, which she quickly swallowed. She was given fresh clothes, and a breakfast of weak tea and dry toast.

"What does Z89 mean?" Erin was asking through the glass.

"Z for Zephyr. That is the name given to this place. The 8 and 9 are the time of my birth. I was born 9 minutes past 8. I'm in the March Contingent - Marcon. There are 10 of us."

Erin giggled, "That means I'm older than you. I was born at 4 minutes past 8, so you're my little sister."

"That's nice," replied Z89. They were both silent for a moment, gazing at each other. Z89 was surprised to see that Erin was bald too. "Your hair – what happened?"

Erin stripped off the cap and black hair tumbled out. Z89 grinned. "Oh, my goodness. You have beautiful hair." Erin thought back to what Edward told her. It was true – your hair was part of you, part of your identity. Suddenly, Erin looked serious.

"How can I get you out of here, Miranda?"

Z89 looked confused. "Who is this Miranda you keep talking about?"

"That is your real name. The name given to you by our mum and dad."

"I don't have parents. None of us do in here," Z89 said sadly.

"You've met them. In the hotel, where you saw me." Erin knew she'd been right in coming to find her twin. This wasn't a good place.

"Those nice people are my parents. Really? I hope I see them again soon."

All of a sudden, Z89 saw her sister's face stiffen and her grey eyes glared back at her through the glass. "I'm sorry, I didn't mean anything," she uttered, worried she'd offended Erin. Erin suddenly whipped round and was pulled away. "Erin!" she shouted in terror. "Erin!"

Another face appeared in her window. It was one of the Orderlies. He looked menacingly at her and then disappeared. Z89 sank down against the door, her face in her hands. She could hear Erin's screams as she was dragged away.

Erin woke to the gentle sound of bird song. She curled up enjoying the warmth and comfort of her bed. Tucking the duvet around her body, she was as snug as a bug in a rug, as her mum would say. Mum will be calling me for school soon, she thought. Closing her eyes, Erin dozed again but was aware of the sunlight pouring in now, breaking through the fragile skin of her eyelids. She finally gave up the battle and sat up rubbing her sleep filled eyes. She gaped at what she saw when her vision was clear. Her bed had been moved and where was her desk? There was a bookcase full of books and objects, a sofa with an array of colourful cushions, a kitchen area with a kettle and fridge. This wasn't her room. "Where am I?" Erin said out loud.

She struggled out of bed, discovering she was wearing pyjamas, and padded around the carpeted room, searching for clues. There were no windows or doors. The room was a box. Ceiling lights glowed like daylight and a dawn chorus of birds came again from somewhere.

The kettle suddenly clicked, and steam billowed. Erin jumped at the tiny sound. Music crept into the room through a small speaker – classical, thought Erin to herself. Toast popped out of a toaster. "This is so weird," Erin exclaimed.

What is this place? Why am I here? Her stomach rumbled in reply. She was starving. Food first and then to work out how to get out of this strange room. After making coffee and buttering the toast, Erin settled on the sofa trying to organise her thoughts. Her head throbbed; a dull ache was pressing around it like a hard band being tightened. Putting a hand to her forehead, something sticky to her touch caused her to sit up. Looking down, smears of blood were etched on her fingers. Instantly, nausea began to invade her body, and she stood looking around for somewhere to be sick. Panic crawled over her skin, her breathing quickened, crushing heat made her break out in a sweat. Erin searched frantically for a door and just when she thought this is it, a hidden door slid open and revealed a small shower room. Erin ran and knelt at the toilet bowl, just in time.

Afterwards, she lay her head on the cold seat and found herself falling, falling through the air. The room was spinning, but she managed to stand and almost fell into the shower. Turning on the hot jets of water, Erin quickly undressed and then relaxed, the scalding water bringing her back to life again.

Later, after dressing in the white underwear, shirt, leggings and shoes she'd found in the shower room, Erin returned to the main room. She tried again to think about what had happened and sank down on a chair near the bookcase. A tiny paper boat sat on one of the shelves and she gasped. She remembered. Miranda. Scooping it up Erin held it on the palm of her hand and the memories came flooding back. The coffin - finding Miranda in the cell – being discovered.

She fought hard against her captors – kicking and punching, using all her karate skills, desperate to escape. Erin finally managed to break free and she ran swiftly down a corridor, shouting and screaming for help. The Orderly barked instructions into a walkie-talkie before giving chase. Rounding a corner, she found two burly men dressed in brown standing waiting for her. There was no escape. The petite girl was lifted easily by one of the men, but she kicked his shins and dug her elbows hard into his pasty looking face. He dropped her sharply on the concrete floor while the second man crouched holding her down, his oily black hair falling across his face. Snapping and snarling like a rabid dog, his spittle dripped into her eyes, yet Erin's fighting spirit did not diminish. She squirmed and bit and punched only to find herself weakening – they were too strong for her. A sharp pain in her left arm forced her to look down to see a needle being plunged into her skin.

Now, as Erin sat nursing a fresh cup of coffee, she found the images in her head became more fragmented. Visions of another room, waking to find her head and arms clamped to a metal trolley; being wheeled into a noisy machine that turned around her body and that was it - she couldn't remember anything else until waking in this room.

Erin's eyes roamed around her surroundings. The comfort here was in stark contrast to Miranda's cell; a carpeted floor, colourful duvet and cushions, magazines and a vase of fresh flowers. Glancing at the spines all lined up on the bookcase to her right, she recognised some of the titles. There was a copy of her favourite book, Anne of Green Gables, something that always brought comfort. So many times she had searched for guidance within the covers, Anne always helping her through the dark times. Removing the copy from the shelf the book fell naturally open to the flyleaf. Erin took a short intake of breath as she read the loopy handwriting in red pen: Erin Nova Winslow, 1 The Close, Newton, Bucks, England, Europe, The World, The Universe. This was her book from home! She could feel the hairs on her arms rising and her skin prickled. Erin reached across for a pile of books and almost dropped them when she realised, they were her sketch books from home. She shivered as an icy breath sighed down her spine. Nausea threatened her again; taking slow deep breaths she took control. What is going on? Why is this happening? How long have I been here?

Another hidden door slid open. Erin started and blinked. There in the doorway was Miranda, dressed in blue. Her twin stepped into the room, the door closing silently behind her. Erin stood and for a few moments they stared at each other, each being a mirror image of the other one. Their hair being the only stark contrast. Erin's long raven black hair framed her elfin face, while Miranda's scalp was covered in stubble.

Time seemed to stop. They each took a hesitant step towards the other and then another step until they were within touching distance. Miranda held up her hand, fingers outstretched. Erin repeated the gesture until their fingertips just touched. Like statues, they paused, breathing each other in. Silence enveloped them like a warm cloak. It was just the two of them in the whole universe for that one moment, and then suddenly Erin broke free from the spell and rushed forward to hug her sister. Miranda backed away towards the doorway, her eyes wide and her nostrils flaring.

"I just want to hug you. Don't be frightened," Erin explained edging towards the cowering girl before her. Slowly, Miranda reached out her hand again and they touched fingers. That would have to do for now, Erin thought and gestured to

Miranda to sit on one of the chairs.

"You have books and pencils and paper." Miranda stood, light coming back to her eyes as she smiled. "These are usually locked away. May I touch them?" she asked shyly.

Erin handed her paper and books and Miranda stroked the pages, then holding the book to her face she breathed in deeply smelling the paper. "Here," Erin said handing her a pencil. "Draw something."

"I don't know how to. We don't draw here, but I love to write."

"What do you do here?"

"We learn from our teachers. We read books we're told to read and then they are hidden away."

"Do you have friends here?" At this Miranda looked scared, her eyes were haunting, darkened pools and her forehead tight.

"We're not allowed to make friends."

"What are you allowed to do?" asked Erin becoming quite exasperated.

"We learn, we follow rules, we exercise, we eat and sleep. We're rewarded, and we're punished. What else is there in life?" Miranda asked.

"Music, films, cartoons, chocolate, pizza, mobile phones ..." she tailed off as she saw Miranda was looking confused. She was rubbing her temples and shaking her head.

"We have music," Miranda said shyly. "I like Beethoven and Mozart."

"You need to listen to some real music. I'll play some for you." She automatically reached towards a back pocket where she always kept her phone – no pocket, no phone. Then she remembered Mal had lent her Cara's phone. What happened to that? she wondered. "Another time, perhaps," she said aloud.

I need some normality, she thought. I can't think straight. My head's really hurting now. What should I do? I know, Dad always makes a hot drink when something difficult happens. It might help now. Standing abruptly, Erin asked, "Tea, coffee?" She turned and stood patiently for Miranda to reply.

Miranda looked up. "Just water please."

Erin brought it over with some biscuits and after a moment's hesitation Miranda took a plain biscuit and nibbled at the edge. They sat, not speaking. Erin's mind was racing with the comments Miranda had made.

Finally, they talked. Erin telling her sister all about their family, her friends, school and the town where they lived. Miranda listened nodding and smiling. She didn't share much of what she did apart from describing all the wonderful places she'd visited, and what she'd learned from books and computers. Erin was surprised they used computers, but soon realised from what Miranda said that the information they were given was limited.

"I'm amazed you have travelled so much. Mum's photos show you in places from all around the World!"

Miranda looked puzzled. "I have only left this place to meet the nice people, every five years. We visit places in the Enrichment Sector."

Now it was Erin's turn to look confused. "How do you do that? You live in this strange place beneath the ground."

"We put on the special head pieces and we're away." Miranda smiled brightly.

Erin contemplated this for a moment. She couldn't understand what Miranda was telling her. Trying to change the subject she asked, "Are you happy?"

"Are you?" replied Miranda.

Erin was beginning to wonder how they were going to get out of this very weird school, where pupils were hurt and locked away, when a voice interrupted them. "As you can see ladies and gentlemen, the girls are demonstrating interesting traits of the human condition."

Bright overhead lights flashed on, blinding the girls momentarily. As their eyes adjusted, they looked around them. The room was a glass box – they were like goldfish in a tank – and all around the tank were rows of people glaring at them. It's like some kind of theatre, thought Erin, growing more and more frightened. Why are these people watching us? Some of the figures sitting on the chairs were making notes, and she strained to make out faces, but shrank back in confusion as she recognised her family. Why were they here? How did they get here? Her mum, Stella and her dad, Patrick sat together, holding hands. Further along the row were Malachi and Cara. The other people, she didn't recognise.

A tall, thin woman in purple walked towards the glass box. She spoke to the audience. "This was an unexpected part of the project, but it's a valuable lesson. As you can see from your observations over the last hour or so …" Here the woman gestured towards the girls, "… each subject behaves very differently and yet they are twins. Obviously the NN2000 programme is not over yet. Our subjects need to turn 18 before that happens. We have more research to carry out. Our thanks must go to Cara for bringing this to our attention, and to give us a chance to adapt our experiment."

Erin reached out to take Miranda's hand. Her twin was a carved statue and not a living, breathing creature and then like a spell being broken she gasped for breath and held Erin's hand tightly. Erin glanced across at her parents; her mum dabbing at her eyes with a tissue. Then she searched for Cara. She looked serene. I knew I shouldn't have trusted you, Erin mouthed at the young woman sitting proudly next to Mal.

Miss Dorling turned to the girls. "It is time to say goodbye. You will be able to see your family for a short time." The rest of the audience filed out quietly.

"Did you know anything about this?" Erin asked the girl beside her.

"No, I swear I knew nothing. After the punishment a few days ago, I have tried hard to be good. I have not had a blue day for a long time, so I thought today I was being rewarded." She smiled. "And I was. I met you, my older sister. I feel complete now I have met you. Thank you for doing this; I'm so sorry about what they did. They control everything. They know everything. They watch us all the time."

The door slid open and Stella and Patrick entered. Erin ran, clinging to them like a drowned sailor to a rock. Her father stroked her hair as he held her tight. "Thank goodness, you're alright."

Erin pulled away and was suddenly aware Miranda was still rooted to the spot. Stella went to her youngest daughter and reached out to hold her, but Miranda held out her hand outstretched like a starfish. Stella repeated the gesture and smiled warmly. "My darling Miranda. We've come to take you home."

"Really? That's amazing. Miranda you are going to live with us at our home." Erin was beside herself with joy.

Patrick gently took Erin by the shoulders and turned her round so she could look into his eyes. "You don't understand love. I'm so sorry."

"What are you talking about? Mum said Miranda is coming home with us."

"Yes, she is, but … you have to stay here." Patrick's eyes began to glisten with tears. "I'm so sorry."

"No, that can't be right. You're joking aren't you. I can't live here, I'll die." Erin turned to her mother. "Mum, tell them I can't do this. Please Mum …" She collapsed at her mother's feet and held on tightly. She was like a small child begging for help, but her mum pulled away from her.

"I warned you, but as usual, you didn't listen," Stella hissed. "I knew how dangerous it was. You thought you understood, but you don't." Taking Miranda's hand, she walked out of the room.

Erin went to follow them, but Patrick pulled her back into the room. "We love you. Stay strong. You can do this. You have to do this for the sake of all of us." Then he was gone.

She lay on the floor and cried and cried. Strong arms encircled her and a voice she knew and loved whispered. "It will be alright, sis." Mal held her tight and soothed her until the racking sobs subsided. "We don't have much time," he whispered. "We have a plan to get you out too. Now we've been down here we have a better idea of what we're up against. Edward will be our go-between."

Erin stared at her brother. "Cara … she … she betrayed us. You can't trust her, Mal."

"Don't worry. I know what I'm doing." Mal took her gently to sit on the sofa. "We need you to find Frankie, we know he's here. Born February 1st. Help him and he'll help you." Mal stood and looked down on her. "I have to go. Keep your head down. Dad gave me this to give you." He passed her a paper boat folded out of a map. Erin held it tightly before hiding it in the waistband of her leggings.

"Thank you," she whispered. Mal turned and left the room. Erin felt empty, as though everything had been drained from her body. She crawled to the bed, burrowing herself under the covers and cried herself to sleep.

Chapter 13

 Z89 looked out towards the sea, overwhelmed by its vastness. She'd seen pictures before and film footage, but this was different. She inhaled the salty smell and heard the waves breaking on to the shore and the water pulling back as though the ocean was breathing in and out. To one side of the beach, a huge cliff towered over her, the different layers of rock sandwiched together. To her left, two pointed hills pushed up towards the sky and paths wound around the hillside. Seagulls shrieked and cried as they fought each other for food at the edge of the sea.

Stella and Patrick drove here just after leaving the school. They travelled in silence with Stella sitting in the back holding her daughter's hand. Now, they sat drinking coffee at a nearby café while she went exploring. As she turned to look back at them, Stella waved and Z89 stared before shyly waving back. There was a lot to get used to. She still didn't understand why she was here and not in school. A lot more to learn about herself and this family. Family – she rolled the word around her mouth, enjoying the sound of it.

An image of Erin came into her mind. I hope she'll be alright, she thought to herself. Z89 knew what was in store for her sister and she was anxious; she was also scared for herself. The only home she knew was the school and even though there were often very difficult times, there had been enjoyable times too. Z89 loved to learn and always excelled in lessons, maths and science particularly. She relished the time for group discussions when she and the others debated and argued and discovered more about each other through their opinions. And more recently she'd found friendship. This was forbidden, but through the debates and time spent in the Orientation Sector, she began to get to know Z42. A blurry image of him came now: his smile, his eyes, his warmth. They touched fingers together and she'd felt an electric current fizz through her body.

Z89 sat herself on one of the rocks jutting through the sand and smiled at her memories. A sudden movement beneath her made her jump and she laughed as a crab edged sideways towards the shelter of her rock. There was a small pool of water there and she knelt to study it more closely. Pointed shells were clamped onto the barnacle covered rock, fat red blobs of jelly wobbled in the ripples, tiny transparent shrimps cantered through the clear water. Z89 was entranced, dipping her fingers into the pool she gasped at the cold.

"Hello." She started as a shadow blocked out the sunshine. It was Patrick. She shaded her eyes as she looked up at him. "A tiny sea needs a tiny boat," he said kneeling and launching a paper boat on to the surface.

They both watched as the boat bobbed about and then fell over. "Oh, that's not meant to happen," Patrick said scooping it up. He fiddled with the folds and tried again. This time it sat proudly on their minute ocean. "Miranda, you need to name your ship."

Miranda thought for a moment. "I name this ship The Butterfly, may she fly across the oceans and return to us safely."

After a short tour of the school and discovering it was vast, Erin was taken uneremoniously to her new rest area in the Nod Pods. Two Orderlies explained to her the rules and she listened carefully. This was new for them too, as all the students in their charge entered the school as babies not as teenagers, so they chose their words with precision, following their orders from Miss Esme Dorling, the school Principal.

By the time they left her to settle in, Erin was exhausted. She couldn't remember the last time she'd eaten, and her stomach rumbled in sympathy. Her Nod Pod was tiny, compared to her huge room at home. I mustn't think of that, she thought trying to focus on what she did have. There was a small wet room with a loo and a sink at the back of the pod. A bed with pristine white duvet, pillows and sheets. The walls were white, the two drawers within the walls were white, even the tiny clock on the wall was white. All her clothes were white. She longed for some colour. That was it – her tour of her pod was over in seconds. No books, no clothes, no stuffed animals, nothing.

"Z84 Marcon, go to the Nourishment Sector, now." A voice commanded.

Erin sat down on the bed wondering what to do, rubbing her itchy scalp where her hair had all been shaved off, her stomach complaining too.

The voice came again stating the same command. Erin suddenly realised that was her, she would have to get used to that number. She'd been born five minutes before Miranda at four minutes past eight in the morning of March 1st.

Erin clambered down the ladder encased in the wall outside her Pod and began to walk in the direction the Orderlies had shown her for the dining room or the Nourishment Sector as they called it here. Entering the space, she was pleased to see other students already in there, seated at long tables. There was relaxing music coming from cuboid speakers in the ceiling. There was the sound of cutlery on china and glass on wood, but no voices were heard.

She made her way to the counter where Orderlies, all in brown, stood ready to offer her some food. Erin was astonished to find the food looked very good. She chose chicken, potatoes and vegetables and then a pudding of fruit crumble and custard. Turning towards the tables she stood confused, not knowing where to sit. Another

Orderly came to her and gestured for her to follow. There was a space at a nearby table. The others glanced at her and then continued to eat.

"Hello, I'm Erin, sorry I mean Z84," she said sitting down between two girls, one with olive skin, the other pale white. One of them nudged her with her elbow and nodded towards the Orderlies who were watching her. Then the young man sitting opposite held his forefinger to his mouth and gave her a sad smile.

Erin understood and ate in silence.

Later, one of the Orderlies came to collect her and proceeded to lead her along the corridors until they reached a huge white door which slid to one side. Erin stepped inside. The high walls seemed to go on for ever, up and up until they hit the sky lights that drew in natural light. To her right, water plunged down over a wall of clear glass. Huge green plants stretched long thin leaves towards her. The Orderly gestured to her to go towards a big carved oak door. As she did so the door opened and a tall thin woman in purple stood on the threshold. Erin remembered seeing her before when she and Miranda were encased in the glass room.

"Come in my dear." The honey like voice sounded sickly sweet to Erin's ears. It reminded her of someone.

"Sit!" Miss Dorling gestured towards a small

chair, and then sat down behind the large desk. She leaned forward, lacing her fingers together and perching a pointed chin on top, she stared at Erin. The only sound was a clock ticking and Erin realised with surprise it was a grandfather clock. It looked incongruous amongst the contemporary furnishings. At least there was some colour here, noted Erin. She glanced across at the bookshelves piled high with books of every size and colour, and in amongst them a pile of her books from home.

"I'm sure you have many questions," declared Miss Dorling as she sat back against the plush velvet high backed chair.

"Yes, I have," Erin said, impatient to ask them all at once. "What am I doing here? Where is Miranda …" her words tailed off as she looked at the stern jagged face of the school Principal.

"All in good time." She waved her hand as if that was the end of the discussion. Miss Dorling silently stared at Erin until suddenly announcing "Because of your meddling, our project has been compromised. However, we have decided we can build something out of this mess and so," she paused. "Trefoil has agreed this could add more to our research. We will observe Z89 … Miranda … just as we have observed you for the last 15 years." Her supercilious smile seemed to burn into Erin's very soul.

Erin went to stand up - to protest, but the Orderly who had remained silent at the door pushed her back into her chair. "For an intelligent girl, you can be very stupid." Miss Dorling sneered at her new charge. "Of course, we have been watching you. You are also part of the project. NN2000 began in the Millennium, when you and 239 other babies were born. 120 of them were brought here and the twin of those children remained in their home with their family."

"Why?" asked Erin. "Why do you feel you can do this?"

"We have the permission of all the families, and they have all been paid very well indeed for the privilege of being part of the project."

"It's not a privilege," spat back Erin. "It's against our human rights."

"Our research is necessary," Miss Dorling explained. "For too long now our young people have become out of control, they are no longer disciplined, they are not taking their studies seriously. Consequently, the country is not creating the right work force. Trefoil came together to rectify this. The British government support us and have invested a great deal of money in improving our country."

During this impassioned speech, the school Principal had risen and swept around the desk to stand looking down at Erin. Then, like an eagle swooping down on its prey, Miss Dorling pushed her sharp face into Erin's. She grabbed the girl's chin between her talons tightly. "You are an important part of this research. Don't ever forget that." She bared her teeth and saliva dripped from her scarlet lips. "But you can be destroyed if you ever question me again, or…" she paused "… or we can destroy your family. If you ever cause any complications or aggravations, you and Miranda will be erased from the project." Every word was punched into the air. She twisted her fingers until Erin cried out in pain.

Abruptly, Miss Dorling let go and stood back. Erin fell in a heap on the floor. The Principal of Zephyr School turned sharply and returned to her seat. The Orderly helped Erin to sit back on the chair as she rubbed her jaw where it had been twisted. She breathed deeply and calmed herself before asking, "When I found myself in that room, my forehead was bleeding and there was a sharp pain like a band had been wrapped tightly around my head." Her head ached at the memory. "What did you do to me?"

"Well done. A good description. Your head was screwed to a metal trolley and then we carried out several brain scans. We were right to bring you in – you have a very high IQ, my dear." The sugar had returned to Miss Dorling's voice. "You have artistic talent as I have seen from your sketch books. Here in Zephyr, we don't normally teach art, but what you have is exceptional, so we may continue with this."

Miss Dorling looked down at her desk and Erin

realised she was consulting copious notes spilling out of a grey folder. She could just about make out some of the upside-down words – Silas Winslow – the name of her grandfather and next to this the word SCIENTIST. Erin screwed up her eyes and continued to decipher the words below – Joyce Winslow – ARTIST. Erin didn't remember either of them; they died in a tragic accident when she was very young. Why does the school have files on my grandparents?

Erin must have sighed as she thought about her family because at that moment, Miss Dorling looked up straight into Erin's soft grey eyes. "This makes interesting reading." She stood and walked to a cabinet. Opening one of the doors, she placed the file carefully on a shelf before locking it. Pressing a small button on her desk, the wall glided across to cover the cabinet from view.

"You will be quite safe here and as long as you follow our rules and do what you are told you will be rewarded. Your sister broke the rules and so she was punished." The thin woman held out a paper boat, as though it was something obnoxious. "She seemed to think it was permissible to write down her feelings, but no we can't allow that." At this she dropped the folded paper into a bowl, struck a match from a box on the table and set fire to the boat. "Feelings and emotions show weakness. Your karate has made you strong in body and mind. This will also be useful in our research. We will test your physical strength as well as measure your intellect."

Erin watched the tiny boat burn. It reminded her of something she'd seen on the television where the Vikings put their dead on a huge wooden boat and set it on fire. A flame seemed to ignite within her mind. This wasn't over yet, she wasn't ready to be set off into the distance, for her family to forget her and for her spirit to rise as smoke up to Heaven. She looked straight at the woman in front of her, held her shoulders back and took a deep breath. "My family will get me out of here. They love me. If they knew what you were really like they would …" She stood with confidence, her shoulders back, her chin jutting high, not scared any more. "… they would kill you."

But, instead of looking shocked Miss Dorling smirked. "Don't you understand! This is what your parents wanted. They want you to be here. They don't need you anymore." The woman threw back her head and unexpectedly laughed with malevolence.

The colour in the young girl's face drained away, her confidence shattered. "You're lying!" Erin sobbed, starting to make her way round the huge desk towards this woman to plead with her. Miss Dorling pushed her away and she fell against a book shelf, some of the books crashing down around her.

"Take her away!" the Principal of Zephyr shrieked; the Orderly cowered by the door, but seeing the anger was now being directed towards him, he strode over to the young girl and hauled her up hooking his hand under her armpit. He dragged her across to the door, which opened as though on cue.

Erin was pushed and pulled out of the room. Another person appeared from nowhere and between them they carried her back to the Nod Pod Sector. She tried to fight back, but it was no use. Once below her Pod, they forced her to climb the ladder, her tender limbs aching, her face sore from being squeezed and scratched.

Once inside she lay down on the bed and sobbed uncontrollably.

Chapter 14

 Miranda woke to the birds singing outside her room. The sun shone through the gap in the long dark blue curtains. Gold and silver stars glittered on the high ceiling. Sitting up she saw her school uniform lying folded on her chair ready to put on after her shower. A gentle knock at the door and the door swung open to reveal Stella dressed in a grey dress and black boots. Her long silver necklace was festooned with red and black acrylic circles. Miranda smiled shyly at her as Stella came and sat on the bed.

"Time for school, darling." She patted her daughter's hand. "How about some breakfast? We have croissants, pain au chocolats, cereal, toast, eggs, bacon – whatever you want."

Miranda gave a gentle smile. She knew she must be grateful, but she was overwhelmed even by the choice of what to have for breakfast.

Stella stood, straightening her dress. "Anyway,

have a shower, get dressed and then come down to the kitchen. Petra's coming around; she'll walk to school with you." Miranda pulled back the covers and swung her legs across to haul herself out of bed, but as she did so Stella let out a cry. "Your legs. What happened to you?"

Miranda looked down at the blotchy marks and blisters that covered her skin. She hung her head in shame as Stella came and sat next to her. "I'm sorry," she whispered. Stella tried to take her in her arms, but Miranda pulled away and stumbled to the window. "Don't touch me, please," she begged.

"What is it, love?" Stella looked shocked. "Have the other students bullied you? Have they hurt you?"

Miranda shook her head. "Please don't worry. I was in the sun too long, that's all. I'll take a shower now." Stella stood and reached across to her daughter, but Miranda backed up against the curtains.

"Alright, if that's what really happened, I will leave you in peace. But you know you can tell me anything." Stella walked to the door and said, "I do love you, my darling Miranda." She turned and withdrew, closing the door behind her.

Miranda was left alone in her room. Feeling scared about the day ahead, but determined to make the best of it, she padded to the bathroom. She admired the sunshine yellow walls, the array of colourful bottles that stood on display and after a hot shower, she wrapped herself in luxurious thick navy towels. I will have to get used to all this colour around me and this comfort. It's all very different from Zephyr, she thought.

The school uniform: black trousers, bottle green blazer and white shirt lay on a chair. Miranda quickly dressed. Looking at herself in the mirror above the dressing table, she sighed. My hair, what am I going to do about that? But her mum had thought of everything and there laying on some white tissue paper was a raven black wig of long hair just like Erin's.

She was ready, but again felt drawn towards the window. Pulling back the curtains, she allowed the sun to enter the room. Blinking from the brightness, Miranda's grey eyes finally settled on the green fields – where sharp stones were jutting out of the ground. A tiny movement caught her eye, it was a butterfly beating its wings against the glass. Pale blue and delicate, it continued to fight to escape, but Miranda could see the insect was tiring. She opened the adjacent window and gently cupping her hands held the butterfly up to the open air. It quivered for a moment as it perched on her fingers and then took off with ease, circling back once before disappearing towards the seven stones.

Taking a deep breath, Miranda closed the window. She thought of her sister, Erin. "Be like that butterfly and keep fighting," she whispered.

"And, so must I," she said loudly to the empty room. "We have to keep going and together we will bring her home." Hoping Erin would find the messages she'd hidden, Miranda checked herself once more in the mirror, something she wasn't used to doing, and then made for the door.

Miranda Winslow closed the door, lifted her head defiantly, took a deep breath and decided to face her new life and whatever the day brought.

Z84 woke with the noise of the daily garment drawer clicking open. The uniform was grey. She quickly showered and dressed. The digital clock in the wall told her she had ten minutes until the bell summoned her.

Her duvet was in a knot, pillows were scattered, the sheet was rumpled – she had not slept well. Z84 pulled at the fitted sheet where it had come loose from the corner of the mattress. As she lifted it to repair the bed, she noticed a tiny piece of paper sticking out from between the wooden bars beneath. Holding the mattress high she reached down and pulled out … a tiny paper boat.

Z84 slumped down on to the floor and stared at the folded paper. Miranda, she thought. This must have been her room. Unfolding the boat carefully so as not to tear the precious paper, she gasped as she read the neat handwriting.

I am so happy. Z42 talked to me today. I hope we will be friends. Life here will be bearable now that I can share

my thoughts with him. This is not how we should be living.
This must be wrong. We should be loved and respected, not
hated and devalued. Together we can make a difference.
Teardrops.

Without warning the window of her pod clicked
and opened smoothly; at the same time, a strident
bell rang out. Time to go. Scratching her itchy scalp,
Z84 wondered what to do with the tiny boat.
Refolding the paper, she slipped it back into its
hiding place. Suddenly, she thought of the little boat
her father had given her as he left. Searching through
the tangled clothes on the floor she soon found it
nestled on a sea of white. Quickly, Z84 hid it with
the other one; there was no time to study it now.

Z84 climbed down the ladder and joined a line
of others, some in white, some in blue and some in
grey. No one spoke. A young man was staring at
her and lifted his hand to his temple, the tip of his
thumb touching the tip of his forefinger. He
turned away with a sad smile.

The line began to shuffle down white corridors
until it arrived at the Nourishment Sector. Here the
line swayed along to the counter, each student silently
taking a tray then collecting bread and jam and tea.

One of the teachers, a grey-haired man dressed
in green stopped her as she went to collect her
food. "Check your uniform Z84. The shirt should
not be tucked in."

Looking down and then across at the others in
the line she realised everyone's shirts were loose.

Grinning to herself, thinking of her own school in Newton, where shirts were always tucked in, Z84 sorted out her uniform. Perhaps though, small moments of me rebelling against the system might shake them up a bit and keep me sane, she thought, turning away from the counter with her food.

Z84 Marcon looked across at the other students, lifted her head defiantly, took a deep breath and decided to face her new life and whatever the day brought.

TO BE CONTINUED ...

ACKNOWLEDGEMENTS

Huge thanks go to my family and friends, especially:

Chris – my friend, my husband, my rock – we have learned to dance in the rain together. Thank you for telling me to just get on and write.

Josh Upton – for inspiring me to follow you in karate, (I still aspire to become a black belt like you) – thank you.

Freddie Upton – for inspiring me with your own writing, your music and for the many paper boats I have found over the years in your pockets, in your room, in the washing machine – thank you.

My wonderful mum, Margaret – thank you for your love and support, and to my amazing dad, John, who I miss every day and whose voice I hear everywhere. Thank you for taking me to North Cornwall over the decades – my second home. Also, my beautiful grandma, Elsie, for making paper boats when I was a little girl.

Annalie Maher – for PR, for friendship, for copious cups of tea and for your belief in my story when I first shared my ideas – thank you.

My publisher and editor - Deb Griffiths, from BAA Publishing – your advice and guidance have opened my eyes. Thank you for holding my hand when it was scary!

My illustrators – Becky Stewart for capturing the essence of Erin's butterflies and Lauren Zorkoczy for reflecting the dark side to this story with your amazing book cover – thank you both, for your beautiful pictures.

A final thank you to all of the lovely people who agreed to read second, third, fourth drafts and for your wonderful critiques – Ronnie, Lauren, Annalie and Chris.

ABOUT THE AUTHOR

Sue lives in Buckinghamshire with her family and Kizzie, a mad flat-coated retriever.

Unfolding the Truth is the first book of the PAPER BOATS & BUTTERFLIES trilogy.

Book 2, *True Tears*, and Book 3, *Igniting the Truth* are available from Amazon.

For school bulk orders please visit Sue's website, **www.sueupton-author.com**

To discuss or book school author visits and to order the Scheme of Work for Key Stage 3, please email Sue, **info@sueupton-author.com**

You can also follow Sue on Instagram **@sue.upton_author**

PAPER BOATS & BUTTERFLIES

Published by Budding Authors Assistant

www.help2publish.co.uk

Printed in Great Britain
by Amazon